BURNING QUESTIONS

By the same author:

Big Questions
Break Me, Shape Me
Breaking Bread
Conversation Starters
Go for Growth
People at Work
Visions
Pilgrims
Gospel End
Broken Cross

Burning Questions

ROB FROST

MITRE
Crowborough

First published 1994

British Library Cataloguing in Publication Data
A catalogue record for this book is available
from the British Library.

ISBN 1 85424 259 8

Produced by Bookprint Creative Services
P.O. Box 827, BN23 6NX, England for
Mitre an imprint of Monarch Publications
Broadway House, The Broadway, Crowborough,
E Sussex, TN6 1HQ
Printed in Great Britain

Contents

Acknowledgements

This book comes out of my experience as an 'agony uncle' in the South London Guardian, and from questions I have wrestled with during walks by Wimbledon Windmill.

My sincere thanks to Meryl Smith who translated pages of illegible scrawl into neat manuscript, and to Richard Smith for accurate and precise proof-reading. Without their consistent encouragement this book would never have seen the light of day!

Thanks to the people on my summer travels in '93 who added so much to the storyline. To David Saville, for hours of valued help over writer's block in Chicago air terminal. To Lou, Pete and Jane, the Martin Brodier Reps in the South of France for endless ideas drawn from their own experience! To Norman and Gaye and Ed in Northern Ireland for providing a quiet space to put the whole thing together. To my wife Jacqui for much helpful advice in Rhodes.

Thanks also to Bob Lawrence of the *Yorkshire Evening Post* for help with the world of journalism. To Richard Herkes of Kingsway for advice on the first draft. Last, but not least, to my publisher Tony Collins.

All the characters in this book are fictitious, and any resemblance to actual persons living or dead, is purely coincidental.

Prologue

Sue Bailey lay motionless in the hushed intensive care ward. She was surrounded by an array of medical equipment. The cardiac monitor still looked irregular, and it had become necessary to assist her breathing with oxygen. The images which filled her mind were vivid and brightly coloured. Some of the faces were unfocused, whilst others were too large or too small. Each scene lacked perspective, and the sounds were strange. Half-heard words, echoing footsteps, and voices all resonating and confused.

A woman was seated by a canal. She sobbed hysterically. She shook with each breath, and beside her Sue saw herself, seated on the same green bench. It was as if this woman wept for all the anguish in the world, as if her tears were a cry to God on behalf of all who suffer.

A man was falling through the stars. She couldn't see his face. But she could see him reaching out a hand to her—as if hoping that she might catch hold of him. As he fell away below her there was no one to break his fall and seemingly no end to his headlong descent. He was falling hopelessly through infinity.

Sue's face looked out at her from picture frames. Some of the faces were happy, others sad, perplexed or angry. As she went down the moving stairway she gazed at the faces—and saw that in each frame she was a different person. Different colour tones, different shapes and different images.

A man in a brown jacket was walking through a wood, and every few steps he would turn and look at her. At first when he turned he smiled with welcome, then when he turned again he looked angry, but the last time his face was covered in tears. She looked at him as he disappeared among the trees and wondered what kind of love this was.

A woman with a towel wrapped tightly around her head was pushing a vacuum cleaner this way and that. The noise of the cleaner was deafening. All around her were piles of cases and luggage. Two small children sat on a packing case. They were waiting. The woman looked up at Sue, and such was the plea for help in her eyes that Sue looked away.

The priest in a black suit and dog collar was digging his garden. All around him were bright yellow primroses. He was whistling a shrill whistle which was as piercing as the whistle of a boiling kettle. And as he dug so more and more primroses appeared, until the brightness of them was dazzling. Was he truly happy? Sue could not decide.

And there were the men in suits. Just two of them sitting at a table, each displaying the same red and yellow tie. They had no faces, but they smelt of strong aftershave and the pungency of it made her feel nauseous. They were huddled together and talking in whispers and she could not make out what they were saying. Every so often one or the other would turn to look at her, and then, almost immediately, turn back to their conversation. They were passing printed documents to each other, and one man, who was slightly shorter than the other, was signing them.

A car, which she felt she recognised, was covered in fire. The red and yellow flames slowly licked around the shape as though moving in slow motion, and black smoke was rising into the clear blue sky. Suddenly the windows shattered and a great explosion shook the ground on which she stood. The thick choking smoke engulfed her. Suddenly out of the smoke, there appeared a woman's face, covered in blood.

Sue felt no fear, and had no understanding of her precarious situation. Perhaps it was the effect of the drugs, or perhaps her body had instigated some protective mechanism which shielded her mind from the enormity of her crisis. If anything, the sensation was mildly pleasurable. She was slowly floating past these stark images, and watching them as a detached spectator. It was as if the complex events which had driven her to this point were gradually unravelling in her mind. Perhaps, at last, she was ready to face the questions which had haunted her for so long.

1
Lonely Hearts

'Single Female, 32, eagerly exploring life and the universe, seeks a fellow traveller who is sensitive, thinking and expressive, age 30–40. Box No 104296.'

Sue leant back in her swivel chair and sighed. Seeing the twenty-four words in cold print on page nineteen of the *Courier* shocked her. She ran her fingers through her long fair hair and adjusted the silver hairgrip at the back of her head.

Sue had always anticipated that she'd be married with a family of her own at thirty-two. She felt disappointed that things hadn't worked out the way she'd hoped. But she wasn't worried, because she felt that there was still time enough.

In a fit of dark depression she'd asked Paula, her friend in tele-sales, to place the ad just before copy deadline. An hour later she'd changed her mind, and would have withdrawn it if she could. But it had been too late.

Sue Bailey was the focus of much male attention at the *Courier*. Her slim figure and short black skirts had been the subject of several whispered male conversations. The soft pink mohair jumper she was wearing really suited her fair skin; it was her favourite, a recent birthday present from Pete. Sue's chunky silver jewellery and fine flowing hair gave her a sophisticated look which the men at the *Courier* really appreciated.

Sue read and re-read the lonely hearts entry, and the words tumbled round her brain.

'Are you that desperate? You . . . writing in the Lonely Hearts column? Things must be bad,' Heart whispered.

'This is the start of a new beginning. You're long overdue some meaningful relationship in your life,' Mind replied.

Jonathan, the thirty-year-old sports reporter, rested his chin on her shoulder and peered at the long line of ads. He was wearing a black tee-shirt with the picture of a red-eyed monster on the back. His belt was fastened by a bull-shaped buckle. It had long horns.

'Looking for a man then, Sue? You must be desperate to look for one among that lot. This is the dross the tide washed up.'

In one swift movement she swung round on her chair and pushed him away with her foot. The blow winded him. Sue really disliked him. He was a bore and she considered him devoid of personality. To her, his most outstanding feature was his acne. It pock-marked his face in ugly red blotches. Whenever he came close to her she shuddered.

'One thing's for sure, I'm not desperate enough to want a prat like you.' Her angry brown eyes pushed him away.

Jonathan smiled broadly, but inside he winced. His inferior education and blotchy appearance made him feel insecure, and he'd always felt second-rate compared to Sue. Deep down, however, he admired her. Her slim figure and fair clear skin attracted him. His brusque attitude towards her was a cover for the inadequacy he felt in her presence, and his jealousy at her success in the world of the *Courier*. He turned and left the press-room trying to look casual.

Sue sat motionless and watched Jonathan leave

through the big black door at the end of the room. Smiling faces peered at her over their VDU screens. Most of the women in the news-room found Jonathan distasteful.

Mind: You are a real bitch.
Heart: Not always.

Sue swivelled back to face her screen. Pete was perched on the end of the desk smiling his warm smile. And then he was gone.

How she hated this place. No wonder they all called it 'The Box'. The building was a large rectangular structure built of brown bricks—unpretentious and without architectural merit. The interior was basic too. Slate-grey decor and lines of cheaply furnished work-stations. The distant hum of air-conditioning filled the air.

'The Box' housed the bustling world of the *North London Courier*, a weekly newspaper of the old school. It was struggling to survive against the competition of several free-sheets which had halved its circulation and cut deep into its advertising revenue. The world 'The Box' contained, like the building itself, was the epitome of functionalism.

Sue Bailey loathed the place. Every hint of creativity and originality had been filtered out of the *Courier's* life by Steve Willshaw, the aggressive new managing editor, who measured everything by his ability to hit advertising targets. This was no quality newspaper: it was a weekly rag with a thin smattering of local news. Sue felt that her Features section did no more than amuse and titillate, and she longed to write something more satisfying. She still missed the previous regime when the managing editor had been a veteran newspaperman rather than a sharp accountant with an MBA. Sue stared at her screen and wondered how long the *North London Courier* would survive.

Mind: Bit of a disappointment, your career.
Heart: I've just not made the right connections.

Mind: Sociology degree. Postgrad diploma in journalism. What the hell are you doing here?
Heart: Surviving. Working. Making my way in the world.
Mind: Pity you screwed up that last interview.
Heart: I did my best. I had a bad day.
Mind: You'll be here for the rest of your life, Ms Bailey.
Heart: Better here than nowhere.
Mind: Really?

Sue's career in journalism had been something of a frustration. A degree in sociology at Warwick University, followed by a one year course in journalism in Birmingham, should have landed her a junior post on a city or regional daily. But it hadn't. Once she'd taken the job at the *Courier*, it looked as if she'd taken it for life.

Her ten years at the *Courier* had passed satisfactorily enough. She'd progressed from cub to senior reporter and on to Features editor without too much of a struggle. Her two year reign as Features editor, with special responsibility for the 'Local Faces' pages, had been quite interesting. But no matter how hard she tried she couldn't seem to cross from the fringe world of the weekly rag into mainstream journalism, where her heart had always been.

She was long overdue a move, and everyone knew it. To stay so long with such an unpretentious outfit was doing nothing for her long-term prospects. She felt that she was good at her job, but it seemed that she was never good enough to get noticed by anyone outside 'The Box'. She had applied for numerous jobs in better papers but had only twice been short-listed. On both occasions she'd been turned down because she had lacked a diversity of journalistic experience. It was a vicious circle. After each rejection she returned to the *Courier* more deflated than before. She needed a break.

Sue turned on her screen.

Mind: You have a deadline, remember?
Heart: So what?

Sue sighed and gazed at Pete's face in the screen. He was looking his sympathetic look again. Speaking those words again.

'That's it then. The end of a beautiful friendship. If that's what you feel. I didn't realise. I can handle it, no problem. When will you move out?'

She wondered how long it would be before the reality of his closeness would begin to fade.

She accessed the document she'd been working on, an interview with a local politician whose parliamentary career could be documented on a postage stamp. She struggled to think of an angle which might prove interesting. More shallow verbiage for middle class suburban consumption.

Her love life hadn't worked out too well. Her romance with Pete, a local solicitor, had recently ended in tears. She'd lived with him for over eighteen months in his spacious upper-storey maisonette in a quiet suburban road overlooking the big oak trees of the local common.

She had first met him at a squash match between the partners in his practice and the reporters at the *Courier*. She'd been attracted to him by his stable, caring personality, and his warmth and genuine interest in people. His closely cropped hair and neat brown moustache gave him a clean-cut, alert appearance. He was tall and strong, and she felt secure when he held her.

The relationship had started slowly, with occasional meals and theatre trips, and gradually developed into a regular pattern of dates and holidays. Everyone at the *Courier* had assumed that Sue would eventually marry Pete, and no one was surprised when she moved in with him one weekend in August following a holiday together in Greece.

Her relationship with Pete, like her job, had exhibited all the hallmarks of functionalism. They liked each other, enjoyed similar interests . . . but there'd been no pzazz . . . and even after she'd left him she only felt a dull ache of loneliness. This hadn't been the romance of the century. But still, she missed him.

Mind: He loved you, Sue.
Heart: And what is love?
Mind: You could have done a lot worse, he was nice.
Heart: Nice isn't enough.
Mind: It's more than you've got now.

She closed her eyes and saw Pete walking alone down the narrow path between the trees on the common. He was huddled inside his old brown leather jacket, and was walking leisurely, as if going nowhere. He looked cold and lonely. Sue felt sorry for him. She hadn't meant to hurt him . . . not this much.

The first customer at the exclusive Michael Jones Sports Centre at seven am each morning is Member of Parliament Cecil Kingston. Even when the House has a late sitting, nothing is allowed to break into forty-five-year-old Cecil's strict daily fitness regime . . .

The white words rolled across her blue screen with ease. She'd been mulling over the Cecil Kingston material for two days, and now, with a deadline to meet, she effortlessly pulled the article together. It always annoyed her that Features articles had to be submitted first. The weekly paper was published at noon on Wednesdays, and her deadline for the following edition came just four hours later.

He swims thirty lengths each morning, and always uses the fast swimmers' lane, before taking a breakfast of freshly squeezed orange juice and muesli in the club restaurant overlooking the pool. The morning papers await him at his table.

Sue had met him several times over the years at constituency press briefings, but more recently at the

Michael Jones Sports Centre. Her personally designed exercise regime took her to the fitness suite three mornings each week, a discipline she found arduous but exhilarating.

The balding bespectacled man wearing a dark blue pin-striped suit, cream shirt, and red tie, was sitting at a corner table in the club restaurant. He was acting as though he owned the place, beaming professionally and sending the waitresses scurrying.

'Mind if I share your table?' Sue was in one of her confident moods.

'No problem. Be my guest,' he stood and pulled a chair out for her to sit on.

He spoke very quickly and in a pronounced public school accent. His eyes narrowed when he looked up at her, as if trying to weigh whether he could trust her.

'How's life in politics?'

'Fine.' He smiled confidently. 'And how's life at the *Courier*?'

'Okay.'

'Only okay?'

'Not exactly *The Times*, is it? Bit frustrating, to tell you the truth.'

'If you think journalism is frustrating, you should try politics.'

'You're not happy then?'

'Off the record?' He raised his eyebrows inquisitively.

'Of course,' she smiled.

'No. I hate every minute of it.'

Cecil Kingston had very ruddy cheeks and he veritably glowed with health and vitality. There was a certain pushiness in his manner that irritated her and she didn't trust him, though she didn't know why. Still, she'd gone on to invite him to be the featured guest on the 'Local Faces' page, an invitation he had accepted without hesitation.

Cecil Kingston told me how he looks forward to his work each day with anticipation and excitement. 'The great thing about this job is that no two days are the same. And, essentially, politics is about making a difference to people's lives. Making things better.'

Heart: Why do you write these lies?
Mind: Because I like to please.
Heart: And what of truth?
Mind: The truth doesn't please—not the readers of the *Courier*, anyway.
Heart: You might as well write fairy tales.
Mind: That's what I do write. Suburban fairy tales.
Heart: With happy endings?
Mind: Not just happy endings. Happy everything. Happiness flows from every smiling syllable from happy start to happy finish.
Heart: And that's what makes you sad?
Mind: I'm sad because fantasy changes nothing, it only provides escape . . .

The formal interview with Cecil Kingston had taken place at his club in the West End. He had escorted her into a sumptuously furnished lounge with deep pile carpets, black leather settees, and a roaring fire.

A male steward in a maroon jacket had served them with tea and toasted teacakes. And all the time, she felt that Cecil Kingston was looking at her, trying to weigh up whether to make some kind of approach.

When she got up to leave he had helped her with her coat, but there was something about the way that he did it that made her shiver.

'I think we may be seeing more of each other in the future,' Cecil whispered. Sue snatched her brown leather document case and turned to go as quickly as she could.

'I'm sure you're going to make progress at the *Courier*.'

She smiled politely, but left without speaking.

Sue looked past the white words and into the blue screen and saw the faces of the many local heroes whom she'd interviewed for her 'Local Faces' page over the last two years. She wondered why she'd bothered. The local actor who'd made it into a TV soap, the local band who'd got a single into the top fifty, a local teacher who'd written a history of the Houses of Parliament, a local surgeon who'd won a prestigious medical award.

She'd had as much as she could take of the hungry egos of her local heroes. None of them had done anything significant, not really significant . . . their claims to fame were as transient as the newsprint which featured them. A week, a month, a year from now they would be forgotten. Yesterday's news.

Her job had become an act. She could flatter her interviewees, show interest in their achievements, express surprise and delight when called for; but nothing really impressed her. Not any more. The same old questions, the same old answers. It was a bore.

Sue was aware that, in her own way, she craved some recognition for her work. She had longed for someone to notice her ever since the death of her father when she was eight. All through her childhood she'd secretly longed for a father who would admire her, applaud her achievements and proudly celebrate her femininity. Her mother had too many problems of her own to notice. And when, eventually, her mother had re-married, it was too late, and Sue felt that she was old enough to make it on her own. Nevertheless, the childhood scars remained, and she still had a deep longing for affirmation.

Heart: And what is fame?
Mind: Adulation. Praise. Affirmation.
Heart: And why do we search for it?
Mind: Damaged egos and wounded personalities.
Heart: And does it heal them?
Mind: It eases the pain of insignificance, but only for an instant.
Heart: And then?
Mind: The craving continues. A bigger applause, a better curtain call, a bolder headline.

Perhaps that was what she'd liked about Pete. His yearning for insignificance. His desire to be a face in the crowd. There was no clamour for applause and no jostling for position in Pete's personality. He was secure in who he was, and confident about what he did. He didn't really care if he never got a place in the partnership of the legal practice he served. His ambition was fulfilled in being a good solicitor, and each case brought its own satisfaction. He could never have been a barrister. He hadn't the ego, or the hunger for success.

Yet, perhaps, that was what bored her about Pete. His stability. His normality. He did nothing without a reason, and went nowhere without having planned to do so. His neatly groomed image said much about who he was. He lacked the spark of unpredictability which she knew she was looking for in a man.

Pete was standing behind her, softly massaging her shoulders. She leant back and looked up into his smile. He bent and softly kissed her forehead. She felt the warmth of his breath. The security of his being there. The joy of belonging.

Mind: You really blew it, didn't you?
Heart: Maybe.

The white words continued to float across the sky-like screen.

> *'And Cecil Kingston's greatest ambition? That one day he'll get a private member's bill which will ban cosmetic companies from testing products on animals.'*

She tapped in the code and instantly her words flew across the miles to an anonymous printing plant which she'd never visited, and to a skilled paste-up artist she'd never met. The copy for her Feature page had arrived with minutes to spare, as usual.

She actioned her desktop printer and the laser sprayed her words onto pure white paper. She never felt that an article was really complete until she'd seen it on paper and filed it neatly in her portfolio.

Her phone buzzed. 'Nice piece, Sue. It was important you got this one right. Last minute, as ever . . . but you made it.' Managing editor Steve Willshaw had been scrutinising her words as they flowed simultaneously across the screen in his office one floor above. One of the first things he'd done as managing editor was to install a computer 'echo' system which enabled him to look into any workstation in the building. 'Can you pop up for a chat? Now if poss?'

Mind: What's he up to? He's never asked me up to his office.
Heart: Maybe he wants to give you the push?
Mind: Or maybe it's promotion?
Heart: Promotion to what?

Sue knocked on his door and walked straight in. It was better furnished than the large News-room where Sue and eight of her colleagues passed their days. It had two potted plants and an oil painting on the wall. His large executive desk with its red leather cover dominated the room. It was his symbol of executive power. Steve was pouring coffee from a percolator in a corner of the room. 'Black or white? I always forget.'

It was a stupid statement. He'd never made her a coffee in his life. 'Black, please.'

Perhaps he'd heard about the split with Pete. Maybe this was a management pep talk designed to show the company's care for the emotional traumas of its employees. She sat down and crossed her black-stockinged legs. She felt slightly uneasy, though she couldn't really think why. She fiddled with her chunky silver necklace and wondered if she'd done something wrong.

Steve handed her a bone china cup and saucer. The coffee smelt delicious. He retreated to the security of the large swivel seat behind his desk and looked at her intently.

'It's time for a change, Sue. You've been writing Features for two years now and the page needs a new look. Don't get me wrong, your stuff's okay but you must be getting stale. Running short of ideas. How do you find it?'

Heart: Tell him you're bored with the whole thing.
Mind: Tell him you enjoy meeting so many interesting people each week.

'I take the good with the bad.'

Steve sipped more coffee and watched her as she flicked back her shining hair. It was soft and reflective against the sunshine streaming in through his long wide window. Her perfume drifted towards him.

'You read sociology at Warwick, didn't you?'

He'd obviously been reading her file. She'd never discussed her past with him before.

'Did you enjoy it, Sue?'

'Yep. Always been interested in what makes society hang together.' She balanced the cup and saucer delicately on her knee and turned the silver necklace again.

'Sue. I'll not beat about the bush. The Board tell me we need an agony aunt.'

'. . . And?' Sue smiled inquisitively, half-guessing what might come next.

'You're nominated.'

'Me? You've got to be joking!' A broad smile lit up her face.

'No, Sue. Features are out. Agony is in. Research tells us that the public wants its local to have a caring profile, and it's up to you to provide it. You know what difficult days we're having—we're only just keeping our head above water—we really need this, Sue. Well, if you want the job . . . it's yours.'

'And if I don't?'

'I guess we could always put you back onto Reporters' desk.'

Sue shuddered at the thought. She'd left the Reporters' desk two years previously. It would be a humiliation to go back there after editing features.

'I'm not sure I could handle it . . . all those problems I mean.'

'You've got a degree in sociology. You're interested in people. You write well. You underestimate yourself.'

Mind: Could you handle the suffering?
Heart: Yes. I'm strong.
Mind: Would you get involved?
Heart: Yes. I couldn't avoid it. I couldn't help but get involved.
Mind: And what will that do to you?
Heart Give my job some integrity. I could write truth instead of fairy tales.

'I'm not sure, Steve.' She turned the silver necklace again.

'Afraid you couldn't handle it?' He took another swig of coffee.

'No, Steve, I'm afraid you won't be able to handle my copy.'

'Why not? You're a good writer. We've never had trouble with your stuff before.'

'If you want me to do this, I'll have to do it my way. If it isn't real it just won't work.'

Sue wanted to write something which would make a difference. She was at the end of writing fairy tales. Perhaps, at last, her work could tell the truth. Perhaps this was the break she'd been waiting for.

Steve drank the remainder of his coffee and secretly wondered if she was up to it. She had a good track record. She was committed to the company. But could he trust her?

'Okay. Do it your way. But do it.'

'When do I start?' Sue flicked back a fine lock of hair that had fallen over her forehead.

'You've got three weeks; and you can take two weeks off Features as preparation time.'

Steve opened the door. The interview was over. Sue got up and walked past him into the corridor.

'By the way . . ." she turned and looked him in the face, 'where do I get my first crop of problems?'

'From "The Box", of course. There are enough problems here to keep you going for months.'

She smiled. Steve had an answer for every problem.

2

Portrait of a Sad Lady

It was six pm. Sue often worked late at the *Courier*. She liked the quiet hour after everyone else in the office had gone home. Most of her creative thinking was done then, when she could work undisturbed, apart from the distant hum of the cleaner's vacuum.

Sue never had to search long for the subject of her next Feature. The buzz of conversation in the office constantly threw up names of people who were in the news or who had some story to tell.

Prominent on her desk was an in-tray labelled 'leads'. Magazines, press releases and memos from reporters were piled high on this tray—and every week Sue would trawl through it in search of her next 'Local Faces' guest.

Sue's main difficulty was to find a range of people from different backgrounds. A run of local authors, musicians or academics could give the page a predictability which Sue was constantly trying to avoid.

Half-way down the pile was a poorly duplicated sheet with the title 'Trinity News'. Sue smiled at the appalling copy and layout. Two black ink lines had been scored beside one of the paragraphs and Budd, the photographer at the Courier, had scrawled beside it 'Interesting bloke'. It read:

Father Thomas, vicar at All Saints for over thirty years, retires next month. Gifts of appreciation and donations towards his retirement fund should be left at the Verger's house before the twentieth of February. The presentation will take place after church on Sunday morning, March third.

Sue put down the magazine. She knew instinctively that Vicar Thomas was to be the subject of her last 'Features' page. By reviewing the changes he'd seen over his thirty years of parish work she could chart some of the social history of the area. It was a nice 'out' piece for her 'Local Faces' series.

She turned off her blue screen and tidied the papers on her desk. She was in no hurry to go. Since leaving Pete she'd been staying at Paula's place, an ugly two-bedroom apartment in a new block of commuter homes near the tube station. Paula had lived alone since her flat-mate got married, and was only too pleased to have someone else to share her space and her bills. Sue had moved out of Pete's in haste, and was staying at Paula's flat as a matter of convenience rather than choice.

The relationship between the two women had been quite cool, however. They shared little in common. Paula had left school with only a basic qualification in keyboard skills, and there was a gulf of status between the girls in Ad-Sales and the staff in the News-room at the *Courier*.

The room full of telephone booths where Paula worked had a louder, coarser and cruder culture than the News-room. You could only survive in 'Ad-sales' by being pushy, and those who could not sell space did not last long there.

Sue and Paula rarely ate together. Sue left early most mornings for her appointment at the sports club, and she often worked late. Paula cooked for herself each evening while Sue survived on take-away pizzas and pre-packed microwaves. It was a strange existence, sharing a home without sharing their lives.

Mind: Going home then?
Heart: Paula's isn't home. It's just a place to sleep.
Mind: Where is home?
Heart: I don't have one. Not any more.
Mind: Was Pete's place home?
Heart: For a while. But not forever.

Sue pushed her ticket into the automatic barrier at the Underground station and strolled to the descending escalator. She was in a dream. It was basically the same tube journey as the one she'd endured to Pete's place each evening, though Paula lived one station further down the line. As the moving staircase descended she felt that life was carrying her downward into a dark adventure she wasn't sure that she could handle.

Mind: Scared about your new column?
Heart: Yes, of course.
Mind: Will you handle it?
Heart: I expect so. I always seem to.
Mind: You'll have no problem answering the questions.
Heart: I hope you're right.
Mind: But will you understand?
Heart: Understand . . .?
Mind: Understand the pain.
Heart: I will listen . . .
Mind: You may listen—but will you feel?

Deep below her in the dark tunnel an approaching tube train rattled toward the station. A warm dusty wind billowed up the escalator shaft.

She felt that this new chapter of her career was going to dominate her life, and that it would begin a metamorphosis that would change her outlook for ever.

The train was crowded. Sue stood silently beside the automatic door clutching her brown leather document wallet and watching the darkness speeding past. She gazed mindlessly at her pale face mirrored by the window, and knew that soon the last remnants of her naïvety would be gone for ever.

She grasped the silver handrail to steady herself as the train decelerated into the station and scanned the waiting crowd for a glimpse of Pete's face. She hoped he wouldn't be there, and yet, simultaneously, she hoped he would.

The train stopped and she was pushed by a crush of bodies embarking and disembarking. She felt again, as she had felt so many times before, the anonymity and isolation of city life; and the feeling sickened her.

Sue's childhood had been such a contrast. She'd grown up in a sleepy Devon village where her father had been the local doctor before his untimely death. She hoped that some day she might return to the slower pace of rural life where people still mattered.

The doors hissed shut, and as the train jerked forward she saw the familiar brown leather jacket turning the corner onto the platform. Before she could look into his face the blackness of the tunnelled wall had reappeared. She must have been mistaken. The lonely ache returned. She stared again at her reflected image, and the puzzled eyes looked back at her.

Sue found the bright photographic lights blinding. Tony Parkes, known to everyone as Budd, was the only photographer employed by the *Courier*. He was going to endless trouble to get the shot that Steve Willshaw wanted. Most of his assignments were stilted groups of boy scouts, borough councillors, costumed amateur dramatic buffs or local football teams. He rarely had the opportunity to set up his two large white umbrellas and array of lights to 'do a portrait'.

Steve was standing behind one of the umbrellas, and from time to time he gave instructions about lighting, angle and pose. Budd made no response, and it was clear to Sue from his knowing smile that he was really doing his own thing. Sue, quite unused to such attention, was embarrassed by the whole process. She was no actress, and her attempts to appear 'happy', 'concerned', 'caring', 'approachable', 'friendly', and 'sympathetic' looked basically much the same. Still, she did her best.

Even as she posed she wondered at the space between the look she was portraying and the emotion within. She wondered if she would be able to convince anyone that she really cared . . . but most especially herself.

Budd peered through the viewfinder and pulled the focus to create a softer image. Her bright brown eyes sparkled in the lights, and the back-lighting created a beautiful sheen in her soft fair hair. He savoured the moment before pressing the remote shutter button.

At last Budd announced that he'd got what he wanted. The session was over, and he began to pack his equipment away.

'Coffee?' Steve asked, expecting her to agree. It was ten am, and he needed the caffeine.

'No thanks. I've got work to do.' She was about to get up from the low stool, but Steve pulled up a chair and sat facing her.

He loosened his red and yellow tie and looked serious. At forty-two years of age he had done well to become managing editor at the *Courier*, though he knew in his heart that his position in the firm was mainly down to his carefully cultivated connections.

'Of course,' Steve whispered, 'there are implications in all this . . .' Steve had recently been through a messy divorce, and, just for a moment, Sue wondered if he was going to suggest a dinner date.

Sue glanced at him inquisitively. 'Implications?'

'You're moving out of anonymity, Sue my dear, you'll become the human face of the *Courier*. The Board recognises that this will make certain demands on you . . .'

'Like?'

'Like opening fêtes and getting involved with charities and being seen in the right places. So we've decided to give you a company car . . .'

'Really?' Sue had never known the *Courier* make such a generous offer to any other member of staff.

'It'll have the *Courier* insignia on the door, of course, but I think you'll be rather pleased with the Toyota Carina I've ordered.' He was talking quickly as if, in some way, he did not fully approve of what he was saying.

'Toyota?'

'I've also arranged for an image consultant to work with you . . .'

'You must be kidding . . .' Sue covered her face with her hands, something she'd always done when she began to feel herself blushing with embarrassment.

'Nope. If we're going to do this at all, we must do it properly. Don't panic . . . she'll just advise you on dress sense, colour co-ordination, hairstyle and make-up. She comes highly recommended . . . she did that new presenter on *News at Ten*. I think you'll like her.'

She peeked at him between her fingers like some mischievous schoolgirl.

'Steve, I thought this was just another piece of journalism . . .'

'And so it is, Sue . . . but if they're going to read you, they've got to believe in you.' The harsh photographic lights were suddenly extinguished and immediately Sue felt cooler and she took her hands down from her face. She reached for her pink mohair pullover and draped it round her shoulders.

Life's moving staircase rattled interminably on, carrying Sue into a different world. She felt as if she'd already travelled too far to turn back and somehow it seemed that the speed of her descent was accelerating . . .

Later that morning Sue stood in Budd's darkroom and blinked as her eyes became accustomed to the red blackness. Some fifteen different shots of her portrait were hanging up to dry around the walls of the small black room. Sue shuddered with embarrassment. As long as she could remember she'd always hated looking at pictures of herself. She hugged herself.

'What do you reckon, Sue. Like them?' Budd looked hopeful. He was hoping for a crumb of praise.

Sue glanced around at the different shots, 'sympathetic', 'approachable' and 'understanding' and the eyes looked back at her.

Mind: Which is the real you?
Heart: All of them, I guess.
Mind: Or none of them.
Heart: I am me.
Mind: Isn't the real you a portrait of sadness?
Heart: Maybe. But it's only temporary.
Mind: Then why try to hide it?

'Is this all?'

'Yep, all the posed ones. But I always shoot extra for my own satisfaction.'

'Can I see them?'

Budd paused. He didn't usually show his extra pictures to people but kept them in a file for himself. These were the pictures he liked best, because they were the pictures of Budd the artist, and not Budd the *Courier* photographer.

'There's only one processed. It's not very flattering, I'm afraid. I took it when you were chatting to Steve!'

Budd pointed to the large tray of fixing solution beneath the dim red darkroom light. She stepped over and looked down. Her red image was floating in the pungent liquid. She was mesmerised by the shadowy face staring up at her.

Budd looked over her shoulder. 'Portrait of a sad lady.'

'Yes, Budd. That's the one I want.'

The darkroom phone on the wall beside Budd's desk bleeped loudly. He picked it up. 'It's for you.'

Sue took the receiver. 'Sue Bailey . . . Yes?' It was her professional voice.

There was a silence, and then a sigh. 'It's Pete. I've had one hell of a day. Any chance of seeing you?'

'No, Pete. Not today. I can't.'

She heard the click as he replaced his receiver. She longed to know why he'd had 'one hell of a day' but knew that seeing him could do no lasting good.

Budd pretended he hadn't heard the short exchange. 'Why this one, then Sue, why the portrait of a sad lady?'

'Because if I was writing to an agony aunt I wouldn't want to unload my grief onto someone who looks like they're in control of their life. I'd want to bare my soul to someone who looks like they're going through misery as well. Someone with a capacity to understand.'

'You're the expert, Sue. But you sure look sad in this one.' His upbringing in Bethnal Green had endowed him with a very laid-back view of life which resonated in the the way he spoke. He smiled at her.

Sue liked Budd. He was unassuming and in his own way he cared about people. She smiled back. 'I wasn't posing for that one.'

Budd opened the door lock to let her out. 'The camera doesn't lie, sad lady. Any special reason for the sadness?'

Sue brushed aside his curiosity. 'Let me have a few copies as soon as you can.' Budd enjoyed her lilting Devon accent and called after her in cheerful imitation, 'Very well, moi dearr . . .'—but she was already gone.

Sue felt good, and when she got back to the News-room she chatted with a couple of her colleagues before returning to her desk. There was always plenty of 'in-house gossip' at the *Courier*, and Sue was popular with the team in the News-room. There was something about her that lifted the atmosphere, and when she was telling some story or relating some incident she was always so animated.

Her mother had first encouraged her to write soon after the death of her father, and Sue's diary had begun as a daily tea-time recitation to her mother. Over the years, however, her diaries had developed into a most private record of her journey through life. In some ways Sue's diary had helped to shape her life, for it had triggered her love of writing and enabled her to put feelings into words.

When she returned to her desk she found a large brown envelope marked 'Courier: Internal Mail . . . Sue Bailey. Private and Confidential.'

She tore open the seal and pulled out six assorted envelopes and a neatly folded note from Paula. 'Congrats. Sue. Your first crop of assorted sensitive, thinking men. Courtesy of ad-sales. PS. Pass on the leftovers to me!'

Sue surreptitiously slipped the envelopes into her bag, and hoped beyond hope that no one knew what they were.

Mind: What are you looking for?
Heart: Someone to love.
Mind: And why do you need someone to love?
Heart: Because without love, I am dead.

Her mind was racing with the possibilities which the letters symbolised. She felt deep within her that at last it was time to clear away the debris of her spent relationship with Pete and to move on. She dialled Paula's extension.

'Paula? . . . thanks for the package. No one knows, do they?'

Paula giggled like a schoolgirl. 'No way, your secret's safe with me. I'm the only one who allocates the Box numbers. Can I read them with you?'

'Maybe . . . Look, after work will you come with me to Pete's? I need to clear out the rest of my stuff.'

'Won't it be a heavy scene, the last farewell and all that? Are you sure you want me there?'

'That's precisely why I do want you there. You can help me to keep things low-key.'

'Okay. As long as you remember to share your left-over sensitive males with me.'

Sue put down the receiver and stared into space. Since she'd heard of the demise of her 'Local Faces' page she'd lost all enthusiasm for it. She knew that the remaining article was going to be a struggle and she had a feeling that this was going to be one of those afternoons when inspiration would elude her. Eventually she took a deep breath and summoned up the resolve to do a preliminary visit with Father Thomas.

She decided to walk to Trinity Church, even though it would take her over half an hour. She felt she needed some fresh air and some thinking space. Some days the air-conditioned 'Box' closed in around her like a prison.

Sue missed the country lanes of North Devon where she'd spent so much of her childhood. She'd 'walked out' many of her adolescent moods along those narrow roads with yellow primroses sheltering beneath the high hedgerows. When she was thirteen and her mother had announced her intention to re-marry, Sue had only survived the trauma by walking the beaches and cliff-tops near her home and seeking a new perspective on life. She never got on well with her step-father. He seemed such a boring man in comparison to her real dad, and she devised many elaborate ways of avoiding his company.

As Sue left 'The Box' she looked up at the dull leaden sky and longed for spring. There were still a few leaves on the ground and the death of winter was in the air. She followed the service road through the industrial estate past the other box-like buildings and cut down an alley-way to the canal. The grassy tow-path was wide and easily walkable. It had been several years since she had travelled this route.

Sue had always liked the canal. It was like another world hidden away behind the rows of squat suburban houses. It was always quieter there, and it made a good escape from the urban maze. Few others found this hidden place, but, for those that did, it was as good a place as any to hide away from the rest of the world.

As she walked Sue gazed at the other people beside the canal and wondered what pressures had driven them to seek out this secret place. An old woman in a blue plastic mac was coaxing a timid poodle to walk behind her. A man, wrapped in a hooded green anorak, sat fishing beside a large open umbrella. Sue paused, and then walked nervously under a low bridge where two teenage boys were crouched with cigarettes.

As she emerged from the shadow of the bridge she saw a woman sitting on a bench. Then she heard the sobbing. It was a heart-wrenching sound. Long gasping cries beyond control. Sue quickened her pace but held back from running toward the woman in case she frightened her.

The old green bench was weathered and scratched and its paint was peeling. The young woman seated on it rocked forward and back and she hugged herself as if seeking comfort. Beside her was a young child strapped into a buggy.

The woman was staring out across the canal. Tears were pouring down her freckled face and a thin streak of black mascara ran down her cheek. The child beside her was asleep. Sue perched on the edge of the bench, not wishing to intrude.

'Can I help?'

The woman turned her face to Sue and, for just a moment, the awful sound of sobbing ceased. They communicated in a silent understanding which was deeper than words.

Sue reached across and touched the woman's hand. The hand slowly opened and grasped her own, squeezing it until the pain was unbearable. Sue pulled her hand away, and, by so doing, ended the silent bond between them. The moment was gone, and Sue slowly got up and moved on. The sound of sobbing followed her.

Mind: You could have done more.
Heart: I did enough.
Mind: And what did you achieve?
Heart: I touched the pain.

Sue walked on until at last the sobbing was gone. She glanced back, but the canal had curved and she could no longer see the old green bench or the woman with her child. Sue paused and looked down at the canal. She was mesmerised by the reflection of the tall dark tower of Trinity Church on the leafy grey water beside her.

A tall ivy-covered wall separated the canal from the churchyard, and the only way through was by a small wrought iron gate which squeaked loudly. She pushed it open and strolled up the shingle path between the graves. She paused here and there, and stared at the faded mossy inscriptions. She was drawn to a cluster of four graves which were separate from the rest.

William Hampton.
Born: 1886.
Died: 1888.
'Suffer the little children to come unto me.'

Stephen Hampton.
Born: 1856.
Died: 1898.
'In my house are many mansions.'

Susan Hampton.
Born: 1858.
Died: 1941.
'Together at last.'

And then a more recently dug grave with a light grey headstone and a bowl filled with fresh flowers.

Maria Hampton.
Born: 1969.
Died: 1991.
'He will wipe the tears from their eyes.'

Mind: Such short biogs. So much unsaid.
Heart: Yet there is enough.
Mind: Enough?
Heart: Yes. Here is love. Here is grief. Here is hope.

The church looked dark and foreboding. Sue had never been religious, and her only experiences of church were distant memories from the village back home. There were the school carol services in the parish church at the far end of the village. And the traditional songs of Christmas, and a crib with a doll inside, and the thought that Christmas was never the same without her daddy.

And then there was the funeral. She still remembered the big black hearse, her mother sobbing helplessly, and the long slow walk to the grave. And, most of all, the soft damp rain covering her face. The very thought of going into an empty church disturbed her. She associated religion with death more than with life.

Sue had intended to follow the path beyond the church to the vicarage, but as she neared the tower she heard the sound of hammering. Intrigued, she pushed open the heavy wooden door and peeked inside.

At the far end of the church, in the Lady Chapel, she saw a distant figure perched on a ladder. The hammering had stopped.

'Can I help you?' Father Thomas shouted impatiently in his broad Lancashire accent. He had felt the draught of cold air as the church door had opened.

'Father Thomas?'

'Yes. Can you hold this damn plastic for me?'

Sue walked over to the ladder where Father Thomas was struggling with a long thick piece of opaque plastic sheeting. Vandals had punctured a gaping hole in the leaded window, and Father Thomas was attempting a temporary repair job. With a hole this size the church would be even colder than usual on Sunday.

Sue climbed delicately up four rungs of the ladder and grasped the plastic sheet while Father Thomas continued to hammer it to a make-shift wooden frame. It was a full ten minutes before he was finished. Neither spoke.

'Right. That's the best I can do. At least they'll know I tried.'

Sue climbed down and he handed the hammer to her. She steadied the ladder while the figure in the black cassock inched his way down. He seemed uncertain of his footing.

'Damn vandals. They'll be the death of me.' He grinned at her suddenly. 'Thanks for the help. What can I do for you?'

'I'm sorry to bother you, but I'm from the *Courier*. I wondered if we could talk.' Sue lifted the collar of her coat as she spoke. It seemed much colder inside the church than out.

'The *Courier*? Really . . .?' His clear blue eyes were fixed upon her, and she was mesmerised by them. Such young, alive eyes.

'Yes, I'm Features editor.' Sue always felt that the title was grander than she deserved, but it usually paved the way in situations like these.

'What a rag. I never read the thing. Waste of time.' Sue heard the emotion in his voice, but couldn't begin to understand what pain the *Courier* had caused him, nor how much the prospect of being featured in its pages would distress him.

Sue pressed on, disregarding his put-down. 'I gather you're retiring.'

'I'm being retired, yes.' There was a note of cynicism in his Lancashire drawl.

'I thought it might make a good story. After all, you've been here thirty years haven't you?'

He turned to face her again. His grey tousled hair was curly and unmanageable, and it gave him a boyish look that was unusual for a man of his years. He had an expressive friendly face that was somehow engaging. She felt that life had treated him harshly.

'I don't need publicity. Just want to slip quietly into

anonymity. Go find someone else to write your stories about.' She heard the cynicism again, but she sensed an underlying warmth.

'But you must have a lot to say . . . after thirty years here. Seen a lot of changes. The readers would be interested.'

'Me and papers don't mix. Not any more. Especially the *Courier*. Now, if you'll excuse me, I've other jobs to attend to.' He snatched the hammer away from her and marched out of the big door, letting it slam noisily behind him.

Mind: What made him so mad?
Heart: You threatened him.
Mind: How did I do that?
Heart: You threatened to expose his failure.
Mind: But it was only a story.
Heart: No. It was his life.

Sue suddenly felt alone. It was getting dark, and she felt very vulnerable. She walked briskly up the wide shingle path to the busy road beyond and returned to the *Courier* by bus. She had never known anyone turn down the opportunity of being featured in her 'Local Faces' column, and she found that Father Thomas's rejection disturbed her. Perhaps here was someone who didn't need fame.

3
Images

It was after dark by the time Sue and Paula arrived at Pete's apartment by cab. Neither of them owned a car, and Sue was determined not to ask Pete to use his. She needed to break her dependence upon him.

'Wait here,' Sue confidently ordered the driver, 'we've got quite a bit of stuff to load, but we'll not be long.'

The driver pulled the peak of his baseball cap over his eyes and leant back in his seat. He'd been in similar situations before. In a matter of minutes he was sound asleep.

Pete opened the door. He was wearing the chunky blue designer sweater Sue'd bought him for his birthday, and when she saw it she had to fight back tears. There were so many memories. He led Sue and Paula upstairs to the flat. The interior was co-ordinated in shades of blue and lemon with carpets and wall-coverings which blended perfectly. The furniture was expensive and well co-ordinated.

'Coffee?' Pete asked, hopefully. He was already opening the lounge door expectantly.

'No, we've got a cab waiting. There's no time.' Sue's

voice was firm. She didn't intend to let this meeting deteriorate into an emotional confrontation.

Paula's eyes were darting here and there. She glanced into the lounge, with its indirect lighting, low marble-topped coffee table and large white sofa. She was impressed. Her own flat was boring and drab by comparison. She gazed into the kitchen, with its beautifully finished white surfaces and pine panelled wall units.

'Nice place you've got here, Pete . . . did you do it yourself?' Paula hoped she might ease the tension.

There was a painful silence, then he whispered, 'I couldn't have done it without Sue.'

When Sue didn't reply he took a deep breath, led them towards the bedroom and opened the door. A tabby cat scampered from its basket and brushed against Sue's legs. She picked it up and stroked it lovingly. She remembered Christmas morning, and the large gift-wrapped box under the Christmas tree, and the sound of purring. 'Tabs', as she called her, was secure in her basket beneath the wrappings. That was fourteen months ago—and now Tabs was full-grown. She'd decided that Tabs would be better off with Pete, but she really missed her furry warmth and affection.

Sue and Paula entered the bedroom. There was a neat pile of cardboard boxes stacked against the wall.

'Thanks for packing it up, Pete. Leave it to us now.'

Sue spoke in her managerial tone. She looked him in the eye, but offered him no glint of affection. She was protecting herself with a thick shield of formality.

'Can't we be friends?' Pete looked pleadingly, nervously stroking his tidy moustache.

'No, not yet.' She handed the cat to him, picked up a large box, and clumsily pushed past him. Paula followed close behind with two more. Sue knew that if Pete showed her the slightest affection she would break down completely.

Pete went back to the lounge, placed Tabs gently on

the floor, and closed the door behind him. Soon the sound of a Brahms' concerto seeped through. Pete often found refuge in his stereo.

The cab driver was still dozing under his baseball cap when Sue climbed into the full compartment and squeezed in beside a pile of boxes. She was nursing a plant pot containing a tall green rubber plant. She slammed the cab door and the driver woke with a jolt. He glanced at the bright red numbers on his meter and smiled smugly.

The engine spluttered to life and the cab pulled away. As Sue looked out of the window she saw Pete silhouetted against the lemon glow of the upstairs lounge. He had evidently been watching her departure. She wondered how he was feeling.

Mind: Why couldn't you be friends?
Heart: I'm not sure I could handle it.
Mind: But you still want to see him?
Heart: Of course.
Mind: Then why didn't you give it a try?
Heart: I've got to find my own identity again.

As the taxi crawled through the evening traffic Paula chatted interminably about the flat, and Pete, and the way that things have a habit of working out all right in the end. Sue sat in silence on the other side of the cab and steadied the swaying green plant. Her mind was full of memories.

She saw them planning the kitchen together—the graph paper spread out on the lounge carpet. And decorating the lounge one weekend—and celebrating its completion with good wine. And buying the marble table at an antique fair—and having to drive home with the tailgate of the hatchback tied down. And nursing Tabs there in front of a roaring fire and stroking her soft, long fur. Tears ran down her cheeks. There were, indeed, so many memories.

Once back at Paula's, with the driver paid off and the cardboard boxes stacked neatly in Sue's room, the two women sat on the lounge floor with their backs to the sofa and drank tall mugs of hot chocolate. The glow of the gas fire wrapped around them as they talked softly in the dimly lit room.

'Nice place, Pete's,' Paula murmured. 'Sorry . . . this must seem a dump by comparison.'

'It's fine,' Sue smiled, 'you've been really kind.'

'I've enjoyed having you here.' She was running her hands through her short ginger hair. 'Being on my own was beginning to get on my nerves. Since Jane left to get married things somehow seemed to come to a stop. She was so full of life.' She paused, and sipped her chocolate. 'Stay as long as you want.'

Sue turned to her and smiled. Her cheeks were red from the warmth of the fire. 'I guess I need some space to sort out my life.'

'Men!' Paula sighed.

'Yes . . . men!' Sue smiled, and as she looked into Paula's grey eyes she knew that here was someone who really understood. Paula placed her arm around Sue's shoulder and stroked the soft mohair of her jumper, and Sue leant against her. They remained united in the silence for a long time.

'How can I ever write an agony column, Paula . . . when my own life's such a mess?'

'Well, if it's any help, you can chat over the questions with me. Mind you, my life's not really under control either!' Paula smiled.

'So can I appoint you to be the agony aunt's official aunty?'

'If you'll have me,' Paula smiled.

'Thanks . . .' Sue sighed a deep sigh of relief. Perhaps living at Paula's might work out all right after all.

Sue had dreaded her visit to the 'image consultant' ever since she'd first heard Steve mention it. She'd done her best to get out of the commitment, but Steve insisted, and Sue wasn't good at confrontation.

The offices of the Warner-Melrose consultancy were in a small turning just off Regent Street, and were situated in a second floor suite of offices above a travel agent. The beautiful young brunette receptionist led Sue through a door marked 'Consulting room' and seated her in a large brown leather chair. Sue felt relieved that she had visited her hairdresser the previous afternoon because she really needed to feel good about herself.

The room was sumptuously furnished; it had designer curtains, bookcases filled with matching green leather-bound tomes, and elegant silk flowers displayed in a tall vase. Three TV screens were placed discreetly around the room and each displayed a rainbow-coloured testcard.

The door burst open and Olivia Melrose swept in. She was a very matronly lady in her early sixties with pure white hair and a grey business suit. She looked austere and formal. Sue registered that the woman wore no make-up.

'Susan Bailey, from the *Courier*?'

Sue got up, as if in the presence of a headmistress, 'Yes, I'm pleased to meet you.' She held out her hand, and Ms Melrose squeezed it formally.

'Please be seated, coffee will be here shortly.' Ms Melrose smiled warmly but she was eyeing her new client with interest. Sue sat back in the leatherbound chair, and the consultant sat down confidently behind the large desk.

'Normally, I like to spend a week with my clients, but because of the somewhat limited budget at the *Courier* we're going to do as much as we can in one day.' Steve Willshaw had thought the consultation expensive enough at £280—and had figured that whatever could be changed about Sue would need to be done in a day rather than in a week.

'One day?' Sue looked surprised. She'd anticipated that the interview would be over in a couple of hours, and she certainly didn't relish the thought of a whole day in the company of Ms Melrose.

The older woman leant forward and looked Sue straight in the eye. 'All I can hope to achieve today is to sketch an outline picture of the image I believe that you should try to develop, and then I will have to leave the rest to you.'

'Fine,' Sue responded, trying to sound confident. Ms Melrose pressed a button in front of her, and, on cue, the receptionist entered with a trolley containing coffee and Danish pastries.

Ms Melrose got up from behind her desk and pulled up a chair beside Sue. As she poured the coffee she appeared to relax and seemed to be making an effort to be more friendly.

Sue gradually warmed to the austere Ms Melrose, and soon found herself chatting honestly about her likes and dislikes, and how she felt about her new role as an agony columnist. At last, when the coffee was drunk, and the trolley removed, and when Ms Melrose seemed assured that her client was truly relaxed—she returned to business.

'Well Susan, if you always thought that women come in all shapes and sizes, stand corrected. They come in four. Triangle, hour-glass, rectangle and pear.'

Sue smiled, and wondered what shape Ms Melrose fitted. The older woman rattled through a speech she'd evidently delivered many times before.

'Each body type has different dietary and exercise requirements. Pears do best with yoga. Triangles thrive on speed swimming. Tennis suits hour-glasses. Rectangles favour aerobics.'

As she was talking Ms Melrose got up and wheeled a small television camera into place and adjusted the focus. Sue stared at the close-up of her head and shoulders which appeared simultaneously on the three television screens, and shuddered.

Ms Melrose returned to her seat behind the desk. She punched a computer keyboard with dexterity and loaded the program which would take Sue into the fairy-tale world of colour co-ordination.

First of all she called up pictures which formed a beautiful backdrop behind Sue's televised image. There were scenes depicting 'Spring', 'Summer', 'Autumn' and 'Winter'.

'The first thing to recognise, Susan, is that all of us belong to one of the seasons, and only one. If we dress in the colours of the wrong season we will not make the best of our natural colouring and appearance. We call this exercise "colour me beautiful".'

This was followed by a protracted process of measuring Sue's natural colouring against a series of coloured 'swatches' which appeared automatically on the screen. At last, after some considerable time, Ms Melrose announced her verdict.

'Well, Susan, my dear. The results are conclusive. You're Spring, and you're a "peaches and cream" person as far as colour is concerned.' She went on to detail the colours most suited to a 'Spring' complexion, and produced a coloured print-out which she urged Sue to treat as her 'Bible' when choosing clothes.

The next part of the 'Melrose' programme included a computer package detailing different hairstyles. Sue looked astonished at the screen as different shapes and cuts were superimposed onto her head. She felt more than a little wounded that Ms Melrose described her newly shaped hairstyle as 'singularly inappropriate'.

Next Ms Melrose turned to fashion, and after a detailed analysis of what clothes would, and wouldn't, suit her client, she made her pronouncement. 'That pink mohair top you're wearing is a disaster, Susan. You're an hourglass, and whenever you choose something you must have that shape in the forefront of your mind. That jumper is better suited to a rectangle with Joan Collins' colouring.' There was a hint of cynicism in her voice. Sue stroked her pink mohair jumper and wondered what Pete would have made of it all.

After a lunch of sandwiches and tea, which was served on ornate china tableware, Ms Melrose turned to the delicate task of preparing Sue to adopt a 'public persona'.

She sat behind her desk tapping different keys and calling up different images onto the three television screens. In a deft and well-prepared speech she illustrated different 'types' of 'public persona' from the 'politician' to the 'pop-singer', and from the 'royal' to the 'film-star'. She explained how each successful personality fulfilled different criteria and how they played the role which their public demanded of them.

She moved on to look at a variety of different 'agony aunts'. She explained why each appealed to a different economic group, and how each one of them had been 'groomed' to satisfy a particular range in the 'market'. One by one the pictures of the different columnists flashed onto the screen, and then Sue's picture returned.

'One of the clearest ways of expressing the kind of personality you want to be is through your choice of clothes. There are six basic types of clothing personality, Susan, and they are: natural, creative, dramatic, classic, romantic and Euro-chic. You need to understand what kind of confidante your readers are looking for, and then dress up to match the image appropriately.'

Sue's mind was reeling at the range of possibilities which confronted her. She felt more confused about her image than at the start of the consultation, and wondered if it was all part of the Warner-Melrose process.

Ms Melrose got up from behind her desk and stood in front of Sue in order to mark a turning point in the conversation. 'And now, Susan Bailey, it's time for you to decide who you are, and what image you want to project. Any ideas?'

Sue gazed up at the face on the TV screen, which in turn, gazed back at her. She turned her silver necklace nervously.

Mind: What's it to be . . . Ms Agony Aunt?
Heart: Classic . . . I think, it spells steady, trustworthy, secure.

Mind: And will you be what your image projects?
Heart: I will try.
Mind: You've not been very steady of late . . .
Heart: Maybe not.
Mind: And will this 'public persona' be the real you?
Heart: I will try to make it so.
Mind: And what if you just play the role?
Heart: I hope I'll remember to quit.

Paula rocked to and fro on the settee, nearly hysterical with laughter. Sue was standing in front of her in a matronly pose and she was impersonating Ms Melrose's 'Colour me beautiful' demonstration.

'That jumper you're wearing is better suited to a rectangle with Joan Collins' colouring.'

'Tell me honestly, Paula, do I really look like an hourglass?'

Paula was too convulsed to reply.

'If you ask me, it's all a bit of a con,' Sue continued, 'I bet if I went to another expert she'd tell me that I was a rectangle with Euro-chic possibilities!'

And then, as sometimes happens in hilarious exchanges, the mood suddenly changed. Sue flopped down on the settee beside Paula and held a cushion close to her as if she was holding Tabs again.

'Seriously, Paula . . . what kind of person should I really be if I'm going to do this agony thing?'

'Well if I were you, Sue, I'd forget all this image junk. I have a sneaky feeling that Joe Public susses out image people for what they are . . . cardboard cutouts. If I were you I'd go for the "warts and all" approach . . . tell it like it is . . . and no pretending.'

'But Paula,' Sue sighed, 'I'm scared, really scared—and I'm certainly not some super-confident Euro-chic.'

'Then that's the person you should be in the column, someone who admits now and again that you're scared, someone who doesn't have all the answers, and someone who gets a bit mad at the way things turn out. Less polish, more reality. What do you think?'

Sue didn't answer, her mind was already composing real replies to imaginary letters. Even as Paula was speaking Sue had seen how she could make the column work. Her daydream was broken by the soft bleep of the phone.

'I'll get it . . .' Paula raced to the phone.

'It's Pete,' she called, a note of disappointment in her voice.

'Tell him I'm busy.'

'I can't, 'cos I told him you were just coming . . .'

Sue let out an exasperated groan and stomped to the kitchen, snatching the phone out of Paula's hand.

'Yes?' she barked.

Pete hesitated. This wasn't a voice he was used to. 'You left a file here, it's got your passport and school certificates and stuff in it. I thought you might be worried.'

Sue relaxed. Her voice softened. 'Thanks Pete. I'll call round for it sometime. There's no hurry. I'll give you a call, okay?'

He sighed a disappointed 'Okay', and she replaced the receiver.

They both returned to the lounge and sat on the sofa. 'Paula, just remember that if it's Pete, I'm out, all right?'

Paula winced. 'Sorry, Sue . . .' Her face brightened, 'Any chance of peeking at your "lonely hearts" mail?'

Sue grinned. 'They're still in my bag. I'll give you the honour of reading them to me, provided I get first pick.'

'Done.' Immediately Paula was out in the hall searching through Sue's brown leather case for the envelopes. She returned triumphantly and fanned them out like a pack of cards.

'First pick.' She pointed the pack at Sue.

Sue plucked out an arty-looking blue envelope and tore it open impatiently. She handed the blue parchment sheet to Paula.

'Read.'

Paula unfolded the letter and cleared her throat. 'Dear Box number 104296, perhaps I could call you "Explorer"? You must be a very special person because I have never answered a "lonely hearts" ad before in my life. There was something about your use of words that fascinated me.' Paula paused, the words were obviously affecting her, and her voice was becoming softer. She continued . . .

'I, too, am "exploring life and the universe", and I am looking for someone to share my journey among the stars. I am too bruised to embark on a relationship just now, but if you'd like to write to me via my post office box number I'd enjoy hearing from you. Write soon. A fellow traveller!'

Mind: Are you really an explorer?
Heart: Perhaps I am.
Mind: And what are you looking for?
Heart: A destination.
Mind: And where will you find it?
Heart: Out among the stars.
Mind: Or maybe within yourself?
Heart: Anywhere, as long as I can find a fellow-traveller.

Paula carefully folded the letter and looked up at Sue, whose eyes were wet with tears. Sue reached out for the parchment paper and unfolded it again. She gazed at the handwriting which was painted with broad flourishing strokes in jet black ink.

'You can keep the rest, Paula, this one's for me.'

Paula smiled warmly. 'He sounds really nice, Sue.'

Sue left her flat-mate to pore over the remaining five letters. At last, after eliminating all the suitors but one, Paula went and made a phone call. 'Brian' sounded nice.

The following morning Sue circulated a memo round all the departments in 'The Box'. It read:

Subject: Agony Column:

My new agony column starts shortly. Problems needed urgently from within 'The Box'. Use sealed envelope and 'internal mail' to my desk. Confidence assured. Anonymous questions welcomed. Please help get this new column rolling!—Sue.

The memo provoked an immediate reaction. Most of the girls in Ad-Sales thought that it was a great idea, and there was a lot of excited gossip about the kind of questions they'd like to write.

The reaction in the News-room was less enthusiastic as the memo heralded a further step away from the local news content for which the paper had once been so famous. Some of them felt that, as a matter of principle, Sue had been unwise to solicit questions from the staff. One of her most outspoken critics was Jonathan, who felt that Sue's new column was going to be a big mistake.

That afternoon he was in Budd's darkroom studying pictures for the next 'spot the ball' competition when he caught sight of Sue's photo in among a pile of matt 10×8s.

'Who the hell does she think she is . . . the Marje Proops of the *Courier*?' He sneered. He was wearing a yellow tee shirt with 'Go for it' inscribed in black letters on his back.

'Oh well, I suppose they all have to begin somewhere.' Budd sat in his battered old easy chair, drawing in a large leatherbound book.

'Honestly, Budd, would you really go to her if you had a problem? Strikes me that her life's quite a mess. What right has she got to tell the rest of us how to live?' Jonathan was always eager to win people over to his side —ever since school days he'd seen life as a competition.

'I don't know. I think she could be good.' Budd stood up, picked up the picture and held it under the desk lamp. 'She's got a nice face.'

'Looks miserable if you ask me.' Jonathan was back sifting through the football pictures.

'But that was the image she wanted . . . moody . . . sympathetic . . . unconfident. I think the picture tells the story.'

'Well I'm not replying to her memo, that's for sure. I'm not pouring out my private troubles to that little bitch.' Jonathan evidently hadn't forgotten his latest brush with Sue.

Budd carefully placed the picture down on his desk, 'Don't be too hard on her, Jono, she's going to need a lot of support over the next few weeks. Maybe you just caught her on a bad day. She's going through a lot of stuff herself at the moment.' There was a softness in Budd's voice.

'Well I hope she's got the guts to put her own problems down there for all to see . . . besides exposing our inner needs to half the population of London.' Jonathan's lip quivered with emotion. This subject had obviously struck a raw nerve.

'If you feel it that strongly, Jono, why don't you do what your shirt says? Go for it—tell her what you think.'

The younger man paused. He felt cornered. 'Okay . . . okay,' he muttered, 'I'll write her a memo.' He snatched the chosen 'spot the ball' picture and disappeared.

Sue, meanwhile, was in the News-room below. She was annoyed that Father Thomas had been unwilling to be featured in her last 'Local Faces' column, and now time was against her. She sat at her desk picking through her 'leads' in-tray, but nothing else seemed quite right. She didn't feel motivated because her mind was already focused on the new 'agony' series. She relished the new beginning that it would bring and felt that perhaps, after all, she was ready for the challenge. The phone rang.

'Sue Bailey's desk.'

'Is that Miss Bailey?'

'Yes.' Sue tried to sound professional and distant when answering the phone at work. There was no hint of her Devon accent when she spoke like this. This professional voice was more reminiscent, perhaps, of the elocution lessons she'd taken in high school.

'I've changed my mind. It's time to forgive and forget. It's been long enough since . . .' The deep Lancashire voice trailed into inaudibility.

'Pardon?'

'I've changed my mind. I was rude to you at the church, and I shouldn't have been. I'll do the interview, if you still want it, of course.'

'Father Thomas?'

'Yes. You came to my church, remember?'

'That's great! I felt you were the right person. Can I come and see you today?'

'Come for tea at the vicarage at four o'clock if you like.' Sue noticed that he sounded much friendlier than when she'd met him at the church.

'Fine . . . fine, I'll be there!' Sue felt good about meeting Father Thomas again. She put down the receiver and picked up her notebook. What did she want to know about him? What would make Father Thomas stand out as the last 'Local Face' she'd describe? The questions she wanted to ask flowed easily, and even as she wrote she got the feeling that this was going to be a special piece about a special person.

4

Hoardings

Afternoon tea with Father Thomas wasn't at all as Sue had anticipated. As she strolled towards the tall vicarage she had imagined a dowdy drawing room, a cosy chat in front of a roaring fire, a china tea service and crumpets oozing in fresh butter. But that was not to be.

'Come in, come in' . . . he smiled warmly and pointed her towards the kitchen. It was dominated by white self-assembly kitchen units which looked cheap and brash. She pulled up a high stool and sat down at the breakfast bar.

'Tea or coffee?'

'Tea, please, Father Thomas.'

'Tom . . . it's Tom.' He obviously disliked his religious title.

The white surfaces were cold and unwelcoming, and the only spark of life was a bowl of yellow primroses beside the window. A large pile of dirty pots was stacked beside the sink awaiting attention. He handed her a mug of instant tea and a piece of crumbly chocolate sponge cake on a chipped brown plate.

Father Thomas looked drawn, and Sue wondered if the thought of retirement was wearing him down. His clear blue eyes were still full of life and humour, however, and she found herself constantly drawn to them. He pulled up a high stool and sat beside her.

Sue took out her notebook and surveyed the list of questions she'd prepared. Somehow they didn't seem as appropriate now, particularly as she'd pigeon-holed him as the 'old vicar' stereotype. There was nothing pompous about Father Thomas but there was a youthful restlessness unusual for a man of his years.

'What kind of piece are you looking for, Sue?' He pushed back a thick strand of grey hair from his forehead.

She quickly looked up, surprised that he'd called her by her first name.

'I don't know, Tom. What kind of story do you want to tell?'

'People aren't interested in vicars today. Especially an old one like me who's well past his sell-by date.'

Sue smiled. 'You don't want to retire, do you?'

'Yes, I do, actually,' he replied emphatically, 'I've had about as much as I can take.'

'Then maybe that's the story . . .'

'Yes,' Tom smiled and rubbed his chin, 'I can see your headline now: "Vicar Quits in Despair".'

'We needn't make it quite that dramatic!' Sue couldn't believe his frankness. He was so unguarded that she felt she wanted to protect him. She played with her chunky silver necklace.

'If you want to write this story, you might as well write it the way it is.' He took a sip of tea.

'Do you despair?' Sue said softly as she took up her biro.

'Yes I do, as a matter of fact. Do you?'

Mind: Do you despair, Susan Bailey?
Heart: I despair at the shallowness of my existence.
Mind: And why is it so shallow?
Heart: So few people to love, and so few who really love me.

Mind: And why so few?
Heart: Maybe my life is flawed in some way.
Mind: Yet you have love to share?
Heart: Yes. Yes.

Sue took a drink of the disgusting tea. 'And may I write this story of despair?'

'As long as you don't add anything, or take anything away.'

Sue tapped the biro against her lip. 'I'll do my best, but I am a reporter!'

Father Thomas smiled but he seemed distant. His mind was reaching back across the years. 'I've been here for thirty years, Sue, and that's a long stretch by any standards. I came here as a very naïve and ambitious young man who was determined to fill this church and to do something great for the people.' His voice trailed off.

'And?' Sue leant forward.

'The response has been somewhat disappointing.' He smiled at her sadly.

'Why?'

'What am I leaving behind me, Sue? A vandalised sanctuary . . . a congregation of elderly women . . . a decaying institution.'

'And where did it go wrong?'

'I made some enemies along the way.'

Sue looked at him intently.

'Anyone in particular?'

'Someone at the *Courier*, for a start.'

Sue bit her biro. 'Who was that?'

Father Thomas smiled and looked away. 'Next question please.'

'What do you regret the most?'

Father Thomas stood up and walked over to his kitchen window. He weighed his answer carefully. 'Maybe I got side-tracked and somehow missed the things that really matter along the way.'

Sue bit her biro again. 'What sort of thing, Tom?'

He turned and smiled his warm smile again. 'The people, Sue, the people.'

It was the following afternoon before Sue found time to write up her notes on the conversation with Father Thomas. She found that the article was easy to write because the material had an honesty which gave it a startling freshness. As she was writing the piece she couldn't help but feel a sense of regret that so many of her previous columns had been dry and stale by comparison.

This was the story of a dynamic young clergyman who'd arrived at Trinity to set the area alight, but who, under the pressure of the years, had discovered that things weren't quite as easy as he'd expected.

Father Thomas had become heavily involved in social action, in the committee structure of the religious institution. In the eyes of the world he had fulfilled an exemplary ministry, but there was an air of disappointment about him, as though, in hindsight, he felt that somewhere down the years he'd got it wrong.

The words were flowing rapidly across her blue screen when suddenly the phone burst in on her private world. It was Steve Willshaw. 'This piece is a bit depressing, isn't it Sue?' He didn't usually criticise her work, and it irritated her that he was reading the material in his office above even as she was writing. It felt like an intrusion into her creative flow.

'I disagree. It's for real. He's local, he's done thirty years, and this is how he sees it. I think it works.' Sue didn't usually speak so confidently to the Managing Editor.

'Can't you brighten it up a bit towards the end, "and so Father Thomas is at last happy in his retirement digging his garden" sort of garbage.'

'I don't write garbage, Steve. Not any more.'

'Leave it to me if you want, I'm going to have to cut it down anyway.'

'Why? It's the usual length.' Sue sounded strident.

'We're going to run your pic and a trailer about the agony column. The copy's being prepared by the firm that's doing the hoardings.'

'Hoardings?'

'Didn't I tell you? Sorry.' Sue felt he was bluffing.

'Tell me what?'

'We're running a poster campaign. It's not very extensive, just local, your face and a caption . . . I'm sure you'll like it.'

'And what if I don't?'

Steve dismissed the question as if it hadn't been asked. 'Remember, Sue, a bit less despair and a bit more happiness and not so many words,' he said authoritatively. Then the line went dead.

It was five o'clock and there was a general mêlée as people all over the News-room prepared to go home. Sue went to the machine, inserted a coin, and watched as the coffee poured down into the plastic cup; she'd decided to stay on and rework the Father Thomas piece one last time. She had no intention of creating a fairy-tale ending but figured that, to pacify Steve, she'd better try to inject a little more hope into it.

After the last person had left, and the last 'goodbye' had been shouted, Sue suddenly felt very alone. Everywhere was quiet. Even the air conditioning had been turned off. She could never remember the News-room seeming quite so still.

She sat and watched the white paragraphs rolling up the screen. This was the most unusual 'Local Faces' piece that she'd ever written. It was certainly honest, and it was real—but perhaps it revealed too much about Father Thomas.

She looked beyond the white words and into Pete's soft, caring eyes. 'Nice piece, Sue. It's one of your best. I like the moodiness. It's disturbing, and it grips me. But what will it do to Father Thomas? Maybe you have a duty to protect him.'

Pete never failed to read her work. Every week he'd laughingly snatch the *Courier* from her when she arrived home and lie on the long white sofa with the paper open at her page. And every week he'd always have something positive or encouraging to say about it. She knew that whatever he said was always genuine.

At last Sue deleted the paragraph about Tom's sense of despair and inserted a softer, kinder piece of prose which talked of 'struggles on the way'. And as she wrote she saw Pete reading her words, and, for just a moment, she felt that she was writing them just for him.

Mind: Does it matter if Pete reads this?
Heart: Yes, it matters.
Mind: Why does it matter any more?
Heart: It matters that he cares.
Mind: And isn't that a sign of love?
Heart: Not the love I'm looking for.

The News-room doors burst open and the silence was shattered. Elsie, the cleaner, dressed in a pale blue housecoat, was struggling to pull the large industrial vacuum cleaner through the double doors.

Sue looked back at her screen and reread the final sentence of the Father Thomas piece. She sat back and sighed. She felt good about the article—like an artist might feel good about a completed canvas. She leant forward again and typed in the words '*HANDS OFF MY WORK OR ELSE!!! Sue Bailey*.'

'Hello Sue,' Elsie grinned. She let go of the heavy cleaner and strolled leisurely to Sue's desk. She was a big woman, her legs looked swollen and painful, and her jet black hair shone with lacquer.

'How are you, Elsie?' Sue was trying to sound pleasant.

Elsie stood in front of Sue's desk with her hands on her hips. 'Thanks for your letter . . .'

'Letter?'

'About that 'Dear Sue' page you're planning on writing.'

'Oh, you got one too? That's good!' Sue leant back in her swivel chair and drew her fine hair tight to the back of her head.

'But I don't write so well, Sue, and I wondered if you'd like to write it out for me?'

'Yes, Elsie, of course. No problem.' Sue was struggling not to sound patronising.

'It's about this.' She dug into her housecoat pocket and pulled out a crumpled piece of paper. It was a handwritten note scrawled on the headed paper of the 'Armour Debt Collection Agency'. It threatened that if she didn't pay the rent she owed there'd be real 'trouble'. It was signed 'James Rowbottom'.

'Can I keep this, Elsie?' Sue whispered seriously.

'Well I've no use for it, that's for sure!' Elsie chuckled.

'How much do you owe?' Sue muttered, as she straightened out the paper.

'Hundreds. It's just mounted up. I can't manage on what I've got coming in. No way.' She shrugged her shoulders.

'Do you live alone or are you married?' Sue was sounding like a reporter again; she sometimes wished she could talk to people without interrogating them.

Elsie threw back her head and laughed. 'Married . . . me? No way. But I've got two kids.'

'Ah, right. Have you got a social worker?'

'Oh yes, I've got one of them. Fat lot of good they do you. She says she might get me a debt counsellor but I don't fancy it . . . would you?'

'I tell you what, if you give me the name of your social worker I'll give her a ring in the morning and see what I can come up with.'

Elsie stared hard at Sue, her eyes wide with anger. 'But I thought you was going to help us . . . not just pass it back to the social. That's what your letter said, didn't it?'

Sue felt embarrassed. 'Okay, I'll come round and see you at home, but get all your bills out. I need to know how bad things are. The truth, Elsie. Okay?' As soon as she had made the offer Sue regretted it. The last thing she wanted to do was to get involved with clients before the first column had appeared.

Elsie smiled a broad grin. She felt she'd won some kind of victory. 'Tomorrow night?'

'Okay. Tomorrow night. And get all the paperwork out. Okay?'

'Okay. You got it!' Elsie clapped her hands as if to signal that the interview was over. She plugged in the vacuum and was soon engrossed in her work. Sue turned off her screen, collected her things together, and headed for home.

It was almost seven o'clock by the time she got back to the flat, and she found Paula in a state of great excitement. She was standing in front of the long hall mirror and trying to see what her new dress looked like from every angle.

'Sue, I phoned Brian and I'm seeing him tonight.'

Sue was unimpressed but she managed to force a smile. 'Who?'

'One of your sensitive, thinking, expressive males. He sounds dead romantic.'

'Just don't forget that you're eagerly exploring life and the universe. I'd hate him to be disappointed.' Sue threw her soft brown case to the floor and hung up her warm winter coat.

Paula stopped admiring herself and turned to Sue. 'Thanks, Sue, I'd never have had the guts to do this if you hadn't been here.'

'I'm really happy for you. I hope you have a great time,' Sue tried to sound convincing.

The doorbell rang and as Sue hurried towards her room she turned and whispered, 'I want a full report in the morning.'

The next day Sue woke bright and early for her appointment at the sports centre, so she wasn't able to hear first-hand how Paula had got on. As she grabbed her coat, however, she noticed a scrawled note taped to the front door. It read: 'Brian's really nice. Tall, dark and dishy. I think it might work.'

Sue enjoyed the challenge of the fitness suite. She measured her performance on every visit and delighted herself in setting ever more demanding targets on the exercise bike, the rowing machine, and the jogging platform. After her work-out and shower she felt really hungry so she went to the restaurant to sample the club's 'full-house' breakfast grill for the first time.

'That lot'll do you no good.'

She looked up from the huge plate of bacon, eggs, mushrooms and tomatoes. 'Cecil, how are you?' She sounded over-enthusiastic, because he was the very last person she wanted to meet.

Cecil picked up the pile of newspapers from his usual table and placed them beside Sue. 'May I . . .?'

'Of course . . . anyway, I'd been meaning to ask you what kind of response you got from the article.' She couldn't really care less, but it sounded genuine enough.

Cecil sat down and grinned. 'Marvellous, Sue. It really did the trick. Everybody's patting me on the head, even the guys at Party Office. I didn't know that they had people reading every paper . . . even the *Courier*!'

'You shouldn't underestimate the dear old *Courier*, Cecil. It goes to places that even the qualities don't reach!' She wondered why he always had to look so immaculate. His blue suit was freshly pressed and his old school tie perfectly knotted. It all seemed so inappropriate for a visit to the sports centre.

'Well, Sue, I really do owe you.' The waitress arrived with his orange juice and muesli. 'Add Miss Bailey's meal to my account.'

'Thanks,' Sue smiled. She was glad she'd chosen the 'full house'. Cecil drew his chair nearer to hers.

'So, you're soon to be famous,' Cecil said through a mouthful of muesli.

Sue looked up from her meal. 'What do you mean?'

'I passed the hoarding in West Street this morning and your face beamed down at me saying "Tell it like it is to Sue".' He smiled.

'Oh, that's awful!' She blushed at the very thought of it. 'Am I ever going to live this down?'

'Oh, but it's wonderful, Sue, and you're just right for it.' Cecil smirked, and chomped on another great mouthful of muesli. 'I told you that you'd go a long way when you interviewed me, remember?' But she wasn't listening.

Sue looked at him quizzically. 'Just right for what?'

He continued munching, then wiped his lips with the serviette and gestured widely. 'For that lot . . .!'

'That lot?'

'The loafers, drifters, losers, and bums who fill my surgery every fortnight.'

'Cecil, that's not a very nice way of talking about your constituents,' she spoke in a deliberately patronising tone.

'I'm just fed up with them all, and with their moans about benefits, and housing, and schools and "how bloody unfair life is"!' He could even swear in a public school accent.

'You really are fed up, aren't you?' She couldn't believe that he could be as callous as he appeared.

'You'll soon see, Aunty Susan. There are limits to what any of us can do. After a while you too will wish they'd all just shut up and go away.' There was an intensity in his tone that said more than the words.

Cecil's education as a boarder at a top public school had marked him for life. He had been bullied mercilessly, and it had left him with such a severe inferiority complex that he clung to his status like a drowning man to a piece of driftwood. For his own survival he desperately needed others to look down on and to despise.

'Any advice?' Sue was hoping to lighten the conversation.

'Just don't get involved.' He paused. 'Believe me, they'll drain you dry if you get too close. Anyway, most of them just get what they deserve, don't they?' Sue made no reply, but hoped that she'd have the grace to quit if she ever got as hard as this.

Sue finished her 'full-house', bade Cecil a hasty farewell, and left him to browse through his pile of morning papers. She sensed that there was a lot of pain behind his hardness but hadn't the time or the inclination to delve further.

She arrived at the tube station feeling breathless and with the first twinges of indigestion. She was already regretting that she had jogged to the station after such a big breakfast. She stepped onto the escalator and began her descent, but as she did so she stared in dismay at the posters beside the moving stairway.

Her picture filled the ten small advertising frames on both walls. Her solemn face looked down at her, and below it was the slogan 'Tell it like it is'. The words tumbled round her mind. She'd heard them somewhere before, but couldn't remember where.

Sue felt that every face on the ascending staircase was turned towards her and that a whisper of recognition was passing from one traveller to another. She suddenly felt very afraid.

She hurried up the road towards 'The Box', feeling physically sick, and longing for the security of her desk. As she strode up the path towards reception she met Steve coming out of the front door with a man in overalls who was carrying a clip-board.

'Ah, Sue, you're here at last,' Steve grinned. 'It's arrived. Your new car. You'd better come and sign for it.'

There in the driveway was a shining red Toyota Carina with the *Courier's* logo emblazoned on the front doors. Sue knew that she'd feel embarrassed every time she drove it. Steve handed her the keys and as she took them she detected a slight look of disapproval in his eyes. All three went for a drive around the block to check that everything was in order.

At last Sue reached her desk and slumped into the chair. She opened the drawer and pulled out some indigestion tablets. It was only ten o'clock but she felt exhausted. She picked up the hard copy of the Father Thomas article and read it again. Sometimes her work seemed to go stale overnight, but this piece was still as good as she could make it. She put the paper down and turned on her screen. An electronic mail message appeared, the same message which was displayed on every screen in the building. She gasped.

I'd like to 'Tell it like it is', Sue. You're a hard, unfeeling bitch and by asking your colleagues to expose their problems to you, you're putting the working relationship of this whole team in jeopardy. Grow up, Sue. You can't control your own life. What right have you to interfere in ours? Jonathan. (On behalf of others.)

Sue's eyes quickly filled with tears. She flicked off the screen and the white words disappeared. Perhaps she wouldn't be able to handle this new assignment after all.

Mind: Do people really feel that way?
Heart: It would appear so.
Mind: And what can you do about it?
Heart: I'll be strong and carry on as if nothing happened.
Mind: And what if you haven't the strength?
Heart: I'll find it.

Sue was wiping her eyes with a tissue and suddenly became aware that Budd was standing behind her. 'I've got my pics of Father Thomas in the fixer. Care to come and look?' Sue looked up into his face, and she knew that really he'd come because he cared.

'Give me a couple of minutes, and I'll be there.'

Sue visited the ladies' room and applied some make-up and perfume. It couldn't disguise her red eyes but it made her feel better, and she knew that the reddened light in Budd's dark-room would give her good cover.

She knocked and entered Budd's province and stood watching him at work.

He had long jet black hair, usually tied in a pony-tail behind his head, with dark full eyebrows and a permanent five o'clock shadow. He was tanned from his recent ski-trip to Switzerland, and his cool grey eyes sparkled.

The pungent smell of photographic fixer filled the air. She looked down at the six shots of Father Thomas and smiled. 'Did Steve get to you, then?'

'Well, he suggested that we needed some nice "happy" poses. Father Thomas with his gardening shovel "looking forward to his next crop of flowers" type poses . . . isn't that right?'

'Never mind, Budd . . . I'm sure it'll do.' She smiled at him, and he responded by sighing. 'I should have talked to you, I'm sorry. Will it clash with your copy?'

'Never mind, Budd, it doesn't matter, really.'

'And Sue . . . don't worry about Jonathan.' He sounded warm and sympathetic. 'He's just immature. Most of us round here know that you're going to be great for the column. Okay?'

Sue felt her eyes welling up with tears again. 'I'm not sure if I can handle this agony thing. Do you think I can?'

'Yep. No problem! And if you ever need a friend, call me, okay?' Budd turned back to his floating pictures of Father Thomas. He was embarrassed.

Sue turned off the main dual carriageway and into the narrow streets of dull maisonettes. They looked bad at the best of times, but it was dark and raining and they seemed even more depressing than usual. There was a paucity of house numbers, and Sue twice negotiated the narrow space between the rows of parked cars without locating 132B Wilson Road. She pulled in and continued the search on foot.

There was no number 132B so she calculated its location by counting the houses back from 140. She rang the doorbell but as there was no response she hammered loudly three times. There was a scurry of footsteps within and a small black girl opened the door.

'Mum,' she called, 'it's that lady!'

'Come in, come in, Sue!' Elsie called from inside, and Sue followed the little girl up the steep stairs and into a tawdry-looking lounge. The girl pointed to a battered sofa. It had scratched arms and lumpy cushions and had evidently seen better days, but it was bedecked with a bright scarlet cloth. Sue sat down.

Elsie emerged from the kitchen wearing a pink bathrobe and large blue carpet slippers. She had a towel wrapped around her wet hair.

'Sue . . . you came. I didn't really think you would.' She sank onto the settee beside Sue and clasped her hand in welcome.

Sue struggled to try to find a comfortable position on the sofa and when she had done so she took up her notebook and biro. 'Okay, Elsie. Tell me the whole story from start to finish.' She knew she sounded like a reporter again.

5
Past and Present

Sue got back to the flat feeling stressed and bewildered. She'd listened to Elsie's story for most of the evening and had tried in vain to work out how much in debt she was. The whole situation was a mess.

She parked the Toyota behind Paula's flat and noticed that the lounge light was on. Soon she and Paula were sat on the floor with their backs to the settee holding mugs of hot chocolate. Sue half-listened as Paula described her date with Brian.

Sue took a mouthful of the warm chocolate and it comforted her. It re-kindled deep childhood memories of bedtime stories on her father's knee beside the roaring wood fire. When the last drop was gone Sue grabbed her notebook and flicked it open. 'Paula, this whole thing's a mess. I just don't know where to begin.'

Paula leant over and studied the lines of figures. 'Are these numbers for real?'

Sue sighed. 'Well she owes at least three thousand and probably more. I couldn't begin to get my mind round it. It's so complicated. Some of these debts go back for years.'

'If she owes more than three grand she'll never pay

that off on a cleaner's salary . . . she's well and truly screwed.' Paula took a final swig of her drink.

Sue flicked through the pages of her notes as if looking for some clue. 'It's her accommodation that worries me most. She's way behind with her rent, and some company called ADCA are hassling her to pay up or get out.'

'Is that legal?' Paula muttered, looking at the figures again.

'How should I know?' Sue sighed.

'But this really isn't agony column stuff, is it? I mean, it's not like the usual stuff in magazines.'

'I know, but what am I going to do about Elsie? I just can't tell her to push off, can I?'

'How proud are you, Susan Bailey?'

'What do you mean?'

'Too proud to ask Pete for help?'

Sue imagined Pete sitting on the long white sofa, his legs outstretched, and his face taut in concentration. He was flicking through the pages of her notebook and scribbling notes onto a clip-board. His mind was racing around the possibilities. She knew that he cared. Elsie had just the kind of problem which he felt he'd been trained to deal with. The scene evaporated.

Sue shook her head firmly. 'No way, you must be joking. I daren't ask Pete for anything right now.'

But Paula wasn't joking. 'At least he could put you in touch with the right people to help.'

Mind: You know he'd like to help you. He always did.
Heart: It's better that I never see him again.
Mind: Why? Scared you couldn't handle it?
Heart: Probably.
Mind: Why do you miss him so much, Sue?
Heart: I miss the security. That's all.

Sue knew that Elsie's problem didn't fit the column, and besides, she had enough problems of her own.

She ripped a clean sheet out of her reporter's notebook and scribbled a hasty note.

'Thanks for seeing me, Elsie. But your problem isn't what I'm looking for in the column. I'm sorry I can't help you. Hope the social worker can do something. See you at work. Love, Sue.'

Sue put down her notebook and gazed at the flickering gas fire, but her mind was far away, back down the years. The sobbing had woken her and she'd crept downstairs. The lounge door was open, and her mother's shape was silhouetted against the roaring fire. She was weeping uncontrollably for her dead husband. Sue knew in her childhood naïvety that she should run to embrace her mother—and should place her arms around her mother's neck and kiss the wet cheeks. But instead, she turned and raced back upstairs and hid beneath the covers, and hugged her teddy bear tight for security. Susan Bailey knew that she'd been running away from suffering ever since.

She folded the paper and sealed it in an envelope. She felt a dull ache within her, though she didn't know why, so she said goodnight to Paula and went to bed. That night, after she'd communicated her sense of unease to her diary, she lay awake and hugged the pillow tight.

Sometimes Paula felt she didn't understand Sue, but it didn't really matter to her, as she was a very easy-going sort of person. She turned on the TV and flicked the channels. She chose an American sitcom about two flat-mates in New York. One girl's self-image was so poor that she spent all her money on facials, tone-ups, sun-beds and beauty products . . . while her beautiful flat-mate attracted a long queue of eligible males. The one who tried hardest seemed least successful and Paula identified all the way.

The News-room at the *Courier* was buzzing with activity. Sometimes the pressure built up during the week until it was barely tolerable, and Friday mornings were often the worst.

It seemed that everyone was busy except for Sue. She was between roles. Her last 'Local Faces' page was safely to bed and she had a week of preparation before having to write her first 'agony' piece. She was leisurely clearing out her desk and filling a large bin with rubbish.

She found the activity strangely comforting. It felt good to throw away the stacks of paperwork which had accumulated over the years; the spent correspondence, the dated leads, and the crumpled pages from her notebook. It all seemed wonderfully irrelevant.

But there were other papers which she couldn't throw away. Letters of appreciation, cuttings of the articles she'd written, and priceless scraps of paper which called up her past: the stub of an airline ticket from a holiday with Pete; a letter from her mother; a brochure about pine kitchen units. They were silly things which, though meaningless to someone else, meant all the world to her.

Another drawer was full of photos of her 'Local Faces'. She flicked through them and smiled when she remembered some of the strange and gifted people whom she'd interviewed for the *Courier*. Last in the pile were the shots of Father Thomas standing awkwardly in his garden, shovel in hand. She gathered the pictures together in piles, placed rubber bands around them all, and dropped them into a cardboard box which she would take back to Paula's.

At the bottom of her in-tray was an internal mail envelope which had lain there unopened for several days. She broke the seal and glanced inside. It contained another smart blue envelope. Sue hadn't expected a reply so soon, and after checking that everyone was preoccupied, she opened the envelope and pulled out the crisp blue paper inside.

Dear Explorer,

I didn't dare hope that you would write back. Thank you. So you, too, are bruised by life. You sound hurt and confused, a feeling I know so well myself. I have lost everything . . . my life, my love, and even my faith. Sometimes I wonder where I can find the strength to travel on.

Since receiving your letter, I've been filled with a new hope for the future. Perhaps, even yet, things will work out for me. Perhaps the pain that I have been through is just a preparation for something more wonderful, yet to be.

I guess I should be asking you what colour eyes you have and what kind of job you do, but instead I find myself fascinated to know more about your journey and where it's headed.

Since my own world collapsed I have been falling headlong through the universe, numbed by the pain of existence. I live in such a place of solitude that I fear no one will ever be able to reach me again.

As I fall through infinity will you stretch out a hand?

Fellow traveller.

Sue carefully folded the blue parchment and placed it back in the envelope. She stored it carefully in the bottom drawer of her desk beside the first letter from her mysterious 'Fellow Traveller'. These letters were not to be cleared away, for they represented the future, not the past.

Just then, Jonathan burst into the press-room in his usual surly way. 'Paper's here . . . come and get it!'

He was holding a pile of *Couriers* which had just arrived 'hot off the press'. Everyone left their desks and crowded around him; they were always eager to read their work in print.

'Well, if it isn't Ms Sue "Tell it like it is" Bailey,' Jonathan sneered.

'What's wrong? Got a little problem with our acne, luvvy?' Sue retorted, brushing his cheek with her hand. Her Devon accent was always more pronounced when she was provoked.

The moment she spoke she regretted what she'd said. One or two people sniggered, but it was clear that most didn't approve. Jonathan was glaring at her.

Mind: You really can be cruel.
Heart: Perhaps it's how I protect myself.
Mind: And why do you need to protect yourself?
Heart: Because I had no father to protect me.

Jonathan dropped the remaining papers to the floor with a thud. His eyes narrowed. He grabbed her tightly by the arm. 'It's time you realised that your wretched agony column is going to ruin the lot of us. This is supposed to be a newspaper, you know, not some shoddy free-sheet.'

'You're such an encouragement, Jonathan,' she spat at him. 'I'm so glad to know that we're all playing on the same team.' She was red with anger.

Sue pulled herself free, bent down and picked up a paper from the floor, and stormed out of the black doors into reception. She walked briskly down the road towards the canal. She needed some space.

By the time she had reached the bridge she was beginning to feel better. Sue had always found walking a great help when she was angry. Life with her mum hadn't been easy after her dad had died. Her mother was never actually drunk, but her slurred speech and quick temper had deeply affected Sue. And all this at a time when she was looking for tenderness and support rather than criticism and correction.

Walking had always helped Sue to distance herself from angry words. And the further she walked the more harmless the words always seemed.

Sue sat on the green seat beside the canal and opened her copy of the *Courier*. Instinctively she opened the paper to her own 'Local Faces' section and stared in amazement at the large picture of herself which filled a third of the page. Sue 'Tell it like it is' Bailey looked questioningly out at her. This was indeed the portrait of a sad lady.

Sue had seen scores of other faces staring out at her from the Courier over the years but had never before seen her own. She didn't like it. She wrote the news but had no desire to become it. It was one thing to expose the lives of others for all to see—it was quite another to expose her own.

Under the picture was one of Steve's exaggerated pieces of prose which heralded the arrival of the new column. It described her as 'a sensitive person in touch with reality who really cares.' It was all hype.

Mind: And are you sensitive, Susan Bailey?
Heart: I feel things deeply, yes.
Mind: And are you in touch with reality?
Heart: Perhaps I am.
Mind: But do you really care?
Heart: I wish I did.

'You never cared for anyone but yourself, Susan—not even when I really needed you.' The sharpness of her mother's words still burned within her. She'd just refused to be a bridesmaid at her mother's wedding.

'Can't you see how important this is to me? Can't you see how much I need you to share this day?' Her mother's eyes were pleading with her. Sue spat the words back at her, 'You never cared for me, so why should I care for you?'

Sue put the paper down and stared at the ripples in the canal. She felt a cold fear enter her heart. She knew that she could never be the kind of caring person that the paper had hyped her up to be. She could never live such a lie. Maybe, after all, Jonathan was right. Maybe Susan Bailey would ruin everything.

She picked up the paper again and looked at the photo

of Father Thomas digging his garden. She was annoyed that Steve had commissioned such a cliché. But there was worse to come. When she scanned her article on Father Thomas she knew immediately that Steve had hacked it down. It didn't read well and felt clumsy and awkward. It certainly wasn't her usual style. The warmth for Father Thomas so evident in her original piece was gone. He was now pigeon-holed as a 'typical vicar' ready to retire. She felt annoyed and betrayed.

She snatched up the paper and walked on past the familiar bend in the canal and through the gate which led into the churchyard. She strode quickly towards the vicarage. As she got closer she saw Father Thomas struggle out with a huge pile of books which he was steadying under his chin.

'Give us a hand, quick, I think I'm going to drop the lot.'

Sue reached over and removed some of the books from under his chin. She followed him to the car and watched as he threw the pile clumsily into the boot.

'Aren't you stacking them in boxes, Tom? They'll not travel well like this!' She gently placed the books she was carrying into the boot.

'This lot are all for the dump, young lady. No good to man nor beast. They represent an era of Christian theology that's gone for ever; they're not even desperate enough for this little lot in Africa.'

'Does the church's theology change so quickly?' She picked up a book that was covered in dust and tried to make out the faded title.

'All but the Fathers.'

'The who?'

'The early church Fathers. I've discovered them again as I've been packing. They're beautiful . . . beautiful. They brought me back to the beginning again.'

'The beginning? You sometimes talk in riddles, Tom.'

'The beginning of all things, my faith. Now. Cup of tea . . . or something stronger?'

'Got any sherry?'

'Never drink the stuff, it's against my religion.' He smiled. 'You look like you could use a tot of brandy.'

She followed him into his half-dismantled study. There were piles of books all over the floor and some old files stacked on two worn armchairs beside the electric fire. He produced two small glasses and a brandy bottle from his desk drawer and proceeded to pour. Sue moved the files onto the floor and sat down on an armchair.

'Only a drop for me; too much of this stuff is against my religion!' She smiled. 'Tom . . . I came with the paper. I wanted to apologise.'

'No need. I didn't expect much, so I won't be too disappointed.'

Sue opened the paper to the 'Local Faces' page and folded it carefully before handing it to him. 'It's my boss . . . he's hacked it around. It's not as good as I wanted.'

Father Thomas stood reading the article with a wry smile on his lips. 'Sounds all right to me. Boring old priest throws in the towel. I'll obviously be better suited to gardening than parish work.' There was an undertone of pain in his voice.

He put the paper down on his desk, moved the other stack of files, and sat in the worn armchair opposite her. 'It's not really why you came, is it?'

Sue flushed in embarrassment. 'What do you mean?' She turned her chunky silver necklace.

'Your work is with words but mine's with people. You can't do this job for a lifetime without sensing when someone's upset. And you, Susan, are one upset young lady.'

Sue got up, grabbed the paper from his desk and handed it to him. 'Sue "Tell it like it is" Bailey. I've taken on something I can't handle . . . and they're trying to make me into something that I'm not, and never can be.'

Father Thomas lifted the glass to his lips and downed

the brandy in one swig. He smiled his wry smile again. 'If it's any consolation, I know just how you feel.'

'You do?' Sue looked into his clear blue eyes and knew that he understood.

'One day you're in seminary studying theology, playing football with the lads, and generally having a pretty cocooned sort of existence. And the next you're thrown into some God-forsaken parish and you're wearing a collar. And the whole world is leaning on you . . . looking to you for the answers.'

'But you're not an image . . . you're not just a picture in a paper . . . at least you're for real.' Sue sipped her drink and savoured the warmth of it.

'Real? In a black suit and dog collar . . . to most people I'm just a uniform. The fulfilment of every prejudice about priests they ever had.' His Lancashire accent was stronger when he felt passionately about something.

'But you're part of an establishment. There's a team of you . . . people to tell you what to do . . . rules . . . precedents . . . training. You're not alone.'

'Rubbish.' There was anger in his voice. 'I never felt so damn alone in my life. When you're telling a woman her husband's dead, or persuading a couple to go on with some broken-down marriage, or trying to help someone to discover an ounce of self worth . . . there's no one there to tell you what to say. You're on your own, lady. Completely on your own.' He twirled the small glass in his fingers. He was irritated.

'But I don't want it. It's not what I went into journalism for. I've not got the experience. This whole thing is just a stupid mistake. All the paper's concerned about is my image . . . and that's no use to anyone, especially me.' Her voice was breaking up.

'Well, young lady, it strikes me you've got two simple choices. You can turn and run or stay and fight. And, if you don't mind me saying so, I don't envy you either.' He poured himself another brandy.

'You're a fat lot of use. I was hoping for some practical advice.'

'Oh no . . . that's your department. Advice. There's plenty of advice around. I don't deal in it myself. I deal in struggle.'

'But there's no such thing as a 'struggle column'. People are going to write to me for advice, not struggle.' She finished her drink.

'People dole out advice because advice is cheap. Struggle costs . . . but at least it's honest.'

'And advice isn't?'

'Well . . . I'm sure it'll make entertaining reading . . . but if you really want my opinion . . .?'

Sue leant forward. Her eyes said 'Yes'.

'You can't really help people from a distance.'

'And why is that?'

Father Thomas turned the glass in his hands and stared at it for some time. 'It goes to the core of my faith.'

'Oh yes,' Sue smirked, 'I'm sure it does.' She sounded cynical.

Perhaps it was the brandy, he was getting angry. 'Jesus didn't stand on a cloud and shout advice. He got involved in the world . . . in the pain. And they crucified him because of it.'

'And how, Father Thomas, does that help me?'

'Well, it's been a model for all my work.' He smiled.

Sue looked intently into his clear blue eyes and tried to grasp what he meant.

'Right from the start I refused to give advice. I saw my role as simply being where the pain is.'

'And how do I do that in four column inches per answer?'

'Well, I suppose you could tell them you care . . .'

'And what if I couldn't give a damn?' Sue flushed with embarrassment, she feared that she had already revealed too much; but then, you did that when you talked to Father Thomas.

He paused and brushed the grey hair from his

forehead, 'Resign immediately . . . or the deceit will destroy you.'

'And what if I can't take the pressure . . . the pain?'

'Oh, you'll take the pressure all right.' Father Thomas smiled his wry smile.

'How can you be so sure?'

Father Thomas smiled again. 'Because I'll pray for you.'

Sue Bailey shuddered. 'Please don't do that,' she said, her voice breaking up with emotion, 'I've got enough problems without God.'

She put down her glass, slowly got up from the armchair and went to the door. Father Thomas wanted to follow her, but remained where he was.

'Why are you so angry, Sue?'

She pretended not to hear him but gently closed the study door and left the house. The sun had broken through the clouds and as she strolled along past Trinity Church she suddenly remembered.

The sun was streaming in the windows of the village church. The coffin, on which was spread a fine bouquet of lilies, rested on stands near the altar. The congregation was singing 'The Lord's My Shepherd', and little Susan Bailey was angry with God.

6

The Column

The pile of agony letters which Sue's colleagues had returned made fascinating reading. They were all anonymous, but Sue could guess from snippets of office gossip who most of the correspondents were.

As she pored over them she felt overwhelmed with sadness. So much suffering in such a small team. She found it quite incredible. Some of the smiling faces who peered at her from behind their VDU screens were, it seemed, living in a private hell.

Sue sat at her desk and flicked through the letters again. She turned over a sheet written in spidery handwriting and smiled . . . she'd recognise Paula's illegible scrawl anywhere! Paula must have known that her letter couldn't remain anonymous because at the bottom of the page she'd written 'Guess who!'

Sue pulled Paula's letter out of the pile and rocked back in her swivel chair, something she often did when she was engrossed. The bustle of 'The Box' receded.

The scrawl indicated to Sue that Paula's short but intense relationship with Brian hadn't been going well, and the 'anonymous' writer was asking whether she should end it. Sue smiled. Paula probably saw her as an expert in ending relationships!

Paula had written the letter late the previous night. She had made three attempts at getting Sue to talk things through with her—but all to no avail.

Paula had the feeling that Brian was two-timing her, but she couldn't prove anything. His unavailability at certain times each week made her suspicious, and he resolutely declined to tell her where he was going or what he was doing.

Sue seemed preoccupied with the plans for her column—and Paula hoped that her hastily scrawled note to Sue might make her think. The two of them seemed far apart again, and Paula's desperate need for friendship remained unfulfilled.

For some time Sue's mind had been active on what kind of style she wanted to use in the column. Most of all, she felt she wanted to be real. Perhaps Paula's question was a good place to begin. After all, her own break with Pete had given her a wealth of experience to share.

'Every relationship goes through its highs and lows, and you'd do well to check out your decision to end it with a close friend.' Sue smiled, and guessed she'd probably be the friend that Paula would choose.

'Ending relationships can be painful and difficult, and a few hours spent chatting the whole thing through with someone you trust would be time well spent.' As she wrote, Sue wondered why she hadn't done that herself . . . why hadn't she opened up to someone about Pete? She'd always been too damned self-sufficient. It was part of her nature.

'Once I've decided to end things, I've found it best to convey a clear message about my decision as soon as possible.' Sue stared at the word 'my' for some moments. Did she really want to make the column this personal? She decided that she did.

'Both of you will suffer much more if you let things drag on

so that your boyfriend doesn't know if you still love him or not.' At least Sue had made the break with Pete clear and decisive. Ending that particular relationship could have taken months.

> *Part of my hesitation in ending my relationship was that I felt responsible for my boyfriend's life. I had to learn that I couldn't shoulder that kind of responsibility towards him at the expense of my own happiness. I came to realise that he had to find his own way in life, and that I would have to find mine.*

Sue felt a wave of emotion flowing through her; she had never sat down and analysed what she'd been going through.

> *I came to the conclusion that I didn't need to be aggressive to end the relationship. There had been a lot of good times and I saw that it would be painful for both of us if it ended in bitterness. Harsh words would only sour the many happy memories we both share. I knew that it was pointless to allocate blame—because, in the end, I'd probably failed him as much as I felt that he'd failed me.*

She watched as the white words flowed across the screen. She felt that she was discovering a new side to her creativity and she smiled with satisfaction as the reply to Paula took shape.

Sue leant back on her swivel chair and re-lived the memory of her split with Pete. It was Saturday morning, and they'd just finished breakfast together. She'd been hiding her true feelings from Pete for weeks. She'd felt that Saturday was the best time to tell him, and had planned to move in with Paula before the end of the day. She remembered Pete's eyes and re-lived those final words again. Her whole being ached.

> *I came to the conclusion that it would be better to send 'I' messages to my man; and that the most caring way of ending the relationship was by being real with him. Rather than*

saying 'You haven't done this or been like that,' I simply said, 'I don't feel our relationship is getting anywhere and I wish to finish it.' An 'I' message led to a more constructive end, and it didn't make him feel too hurt.

She looked at the word 'hurt' and wondered if she could have made it any easier for Pete.

My 'I' message showed that I was prepared to take responsibility for my own feelings and actions. My boyfriend had already guessed that things weren't right between us, and you'll probably find that the same is true in your situation. He may well prefer to know how you really feel. He may even agree with your decision.

In her mind Sue looked across the breakfast table and noticed how pale Pete looked, and how the colour had drained from his face. Whilst he'd been aware that things weren't right between them, he'd no idea how serious the situation had become. He was devastated, and wanted to give her well-argued reasons for continuing the relationship . . . but he hadn't the heart. He simply sat and looked at her, and there was love in his eyes.

Sue wished she hadn't been drawn into saying so much at that last breakfast with Pete. She'd filled the silences with a rambling explanation of her feelings. She had become confused and irrational.

'When was the last time we actually sat down and talked to each other . . . when did we really share anything at any depth . . . we just can't seem to communicate. There's a huge distance between us . . . it's all pointless.' She'd run out of the room in tears.

She typed again, *'Try to be as caring and constructive as you can, and don't criticise or blame your boyfriend. At such an emotive time you could deeply hurt him.'*

Sue looked into Pete's eyes, and saw the pain. She knew that she'd never fully understand what she'd done to him. She pulled herself back to the white flowing words.

'It is in both your interests that you finish the relationship if it isn't working. I felt that it was better to face pain now rather than to drift into a lifetime of misery.'

She tapped out the code to activate her printer, then sat back in the chair and read the words as they appeared. The emotion of what she'd written touched her, and she wondered if it would touch her readers too.

The week of waiting between copy deadline and publication day seemed to last for ever. On Wednesday, like every Wednesday, Jonathan entered the news-room with the pile of *Couriers* 'hot off the press' and held them in his arms. Sue Bailey hung back because she'd dreaded this moment. She knew that there'd be an instant reaction to her first column from the rest of the team at 'The Box'. If they didn't like something they had ways of saying so; a quick change of subject, a glance away, an 'I thought your piece was okay'. Sue was looking for affirmation, but even more she wanted to know how they really felt.

After he'd distributed the papers Jonathan took his copy over to his desk. The room was silent except for the rustle of turning pages. Jonathan leant back on his chair and placed his feet on the desk. He held the paper wide open in front of him. Minutes later he breathed out a loud sigh.

'Well, Sue, you've really excelled yourself, I must say . . . what a load of rubbish!' His voice was full of sarcasm.

Disjointed voices from around the room echoed in reply as if rehearsed. 'Shut your face . . .' '. . . don't let him get you down, Sue . . . it's good . . .' 'the punters will love it, Sue . . .' 'thank God it's for real . . .' Susan Bailey looked at her page spread out on the desk before her and smiled in satisfaction. Perhaps it would work out all right, after all.

Steve was delighted. The following day Sue sat in his office and listened to a stream of praise. 'You're brilliant,

Sue, we've never had a reaction like it. Look at these advertisers' messages. The Board like it too . . . keep up the good work!' He droned on and on, but she remained unconvinced that he was sincere. And who was the 'Board'? This invisible world within the *Courier*. Everyone heard Steve speak of the 'Board', but no-one seemed to know who they were, or what their agenda was.

As the weeks went by Sue's column became an important part of the *Courier's* life. The response seemed to grow with every issue. A three-drawer filing cabinet was installed beside her desk, and each day's mail was opened and filed by a junior. Sue would trawl through it and pick out the letters she wanted to answer.

She found the work engrossing, and all her energy was absorbed in reading the letters of her invisible correspondents. But all the time she was looking for letters which echoed the suffering that she had known in her own life.

Elsie was cooking rice and beans when she heard the hammering on the door, and she was in no hurry to answer it. At last she turned the gas down low, wiped her hands on her old dressing gown, and went downstairs to the door.

When she saw who was there her heart sank. James Rowbottom from the Armour Debt Collection Agency stood with a file in his hand. 'Cashed your Giro, then?' he demanded. He barged past her impatiently. She followed him up the stairs and into the lounge. 'I need the money for the kids—we've got to eat.'

'That's your problem, lady—hand it over now.'

'I can't—I can't,' Elsie moaned, 'It's already spent.'

James Rowbottom dropped his file to the ground and grasped her dressing gown by the collar, 'Stop messing with me, lady.'

She pushed him away hard and he swung back

and punched her cheek. She laughed hysterically; he punched again, but this time with all his might.

The pile of mail which accumulated each week threw up plenty of questions for the following week's column, and Sue could afford to be selective.

One morning her eye was drawn to a neatly typed letter without a signature or an address. It described the distance between a young woman and her husband and how they couldn't talk together any more.

Sue's words flowed easily in reply. *'There can be a breakdown of good communication at any stage in a relationship and it can happen suddenly or deteriorate over a period of months. It's an indication that things are not right.'* This, above all, had signalled to Sue that her life with Pete was over.

Sometimes couples drift apart and discover that they have very little in common. At least, that's what happened with me. I suddenly realised that we were no longer sharing the same interests nor working together toward the same goals. Our level of communication had sunk to the level of the functional. There was nothing deeper than 'pass the marmalade'!

It had been months since she'd shared anything real with Pete. *'It's possible that your husband doesn't realise that you have a problem. His needs in the marriage may be completely fulfilled.'* Sue suspected that this was the case with Pete, who didn't seem to need anything deeper in the relationship.

'If you are unhappy about this lack of communication you must try to explain to him how you feel. Help him to realise that you both have a problem which needs to be tackled together.' Why hadn't she done this with Pete? Perhaps, in hindsight, they could have established something more fulfilling again.

It demands effort and commitment from both partners to reverse this trend. Thinking, speaking and acting positively towards your partner is likely to help you overcome this problem.

I know that a relationship without any depth of sharing is very unsatisfying. Looking back, I wish that I'd invested more time and energy into developing a deeper level of communication instead of longing for new romantic feelings.

'So this is where it all happens.'

Sue looked up from her desk. She'd been deep in concentration, and the voice startled her.

'Tom!' she exclaimed, 'Great to see you . . . coffee?'

She pulled up a spare swivel chair beside her and shouted to one of the juniors to bring over some coffee. Father Thomas looked different. He looked so much younger . . . and so much happier. He was wearing an open necked check shirt and a chunky green sweater which really suited him. He was smiling.

'I just dropped by to see how you're coping. How's the column going?'

'Fine, just fine. Look at all the mail!' She felt that the response proved that he'd been wrong. The column was important to people, she could help them—even if it was from a distance.

'I'm pleased for you.' His blue eyes looked at her with tenderness. He knew that Sue's column was the portrait of a sad lady.

Mind: And why do his blue eyes disturb you?
Heart: Because they see me.
Mind: And what do they see?
Heart: They see the truth behind the fairy-tale.
Mind: And what is truth?
Heart: That this column is for me, and not for them at all.

The coffee arrived. He told her about his first four weeks of retirement and how the pressure was off. He felt much better without the weight of the institution around his neck.

'What are your plans now, Tom?' She still liked him,

despite the tension between them the last time they had met.

'I've taken up walking!' He sipped his coffee, but was studying her reaction out of the corner of his eye.

'Walking—hiking—the Lake District . . . all that sort of stuff?'

'No, just walking.' He smiled.

'And . . . ?'

'I never realised how many people there are down by the canal.'

'What do you mean?'

'I was so busy with that church all those years, keeping the place open, and running the committees . . . while there were all those people down by the canal.'

'Yes, I've seen some of them.' Sue remembered the sobbing woman on the bench.

'It seems to be the place where people go to escape or to think.' He drank some more coffee and placed the plastic cup gently down.

'So . . . what's new?' Sometimes she wished Father Thomas would get to the point.

'Well Sue, I've become a priest again, but this time without the collar.'

'Priest . . .?'

'I've been talking to the people down by the canal.'

'And you're enjoying it?' Sue leant towards him.

'I'm rediscovering what it's all about.'

'Well, if ever I'm in trouble—I'll know where to find you!'

'Yes, I'm usually down by the canal every afternoon. Do come, if ever you need to.'

She smiled sympathetically, but knew she'd never need to go.

Father Thomas drained the last drop of coffee from his cup, smiled warmly, said 'I'll see you,' and left as suddenly as he had arrived. He wondered if he'd been an intrusion. Jonathan almost collided with him at the double doors and apologised loudly.

'Been making your confession, Sue?' he called, so that everyone could hear.

Sue made no reply.

'Anyway, Ms Bailey, there's an urgent internal envelope here for you. I picked it up in Ad Sales.' He dropped it on her desk as he passed but she didn't look up. She prised it open: it contained one single blue envelope. If only Jonathan knew what it was. She smiled to herself, checked that no-one was looking and then opened it impatiently.

Dear Explorer,

Thanks for your latest letter. So you've experienced heartache and confusion, too—and you, like me, have been wounded in love.

I am an artist, and like most artists, I'm a sensitive kind of guy. It seems that some people can take the knocks and disappointments of life more easily than people like us.

I, like you, have been struggling to find a new purpose for my life. My work, though fulfilling, does not really satisfy me. My friends, though faithful, leave something missing. How can I cope with these feelings of loneliness . . . and how can I find my way again?

Fellow Traveller.

Sue folded the letter carefully and placed it back in the envelope. She hid it in the bottom of her desk with the others, and turned on her blue screen.

Loneliness is a painful and depressing experience and it is sometimes hard to know how to survive it.

There is 'emotional loneliness' which occurs when someone lacks an intimate relationship with a spouse, parent or special friend. But there is also 'social loneliness' when a person doesn't feel part of the community.

Many feel that 'no one has time' for them. Others express dissatisfaction with singles' clubs because they feel pressurised into romantic relationships for which they feel unprepared.

Psychologists tell us that even people with a crowd of friends can feel deeply lonely. I share your feelings of loneliness. I guess that people look at me and think of me as 'successful' or 'popular', but in fact, I am very much alone.

Sue knew loneliness. She knew it when she descended the station escalator. She knew it when she sat alone in the flat, and she knew it when she thought of Pete.

It was the companionship she missed most of all. Lying in his arms on the long white sofa and listening to his soft voice. He was a strong and gentle man, and being held by him had been one of the most beautiful and sensuous experiences she had ever known. Perhaps this had been love, perhaps it hadn't.

When I feel lonely I know that I must fight the self pity that fills my mind. I tend to brood over my situation and become dominated by feelings of failure in the relationships of my life. It's a real struggle to stop thinking about myself and to try and start thinking about the needs of others.

As she wrote Sue knew the advice was just for her.

Her phone bleeped. It was Steve. After his initial interest in the column, he hadn't spoken to her for weeks.

'Sue—good stuff last week. The Board have been discussing you.' He sounded slightly embarrassed.

'The Board? They've been discussing me?'

'Yes, and they want to meet you. To say thanks personally.'

Sue smiled. So, she was going to meet this mysterious Board at last. 'Where and when?'

'The Grange country club, Wednesday next, for lunch.'

'I'll be there.' She would look forward to it. She savoured the moment; it seemed that her career was making progress at last.

Sue drove up the long driveway to the ivy covered frontage of The Grange, wondering what she'd let herself in for. A waiter greeted her at the door and led her into the Victorian dining room which overlooked a walled garden. Sue looked around for a group of businessmen in the crowded restaurant. Another waiter approached her. 'Miss Bailey? Your table is in the corner of the Garden Room. Please follow me.'

The window table in the empty room was only set for two; and there, standing to greet her, was Cecil Kingston, MP. The waiter pulled out her chair and she sat down. He spread the napkin out for her and quietly retreated.

'Sue, how good of you to come. I am grateful.'

Sue glanced at Cecil quizzically. 'Board?'

'Yes, Sue—I own the *Courier*, and therefore I am the Board.'

He reached across the table and covered her hand with his and stroked it with his thumb.

Sue shuddered.

'And now, my dear—have I ever told you how attractive I find you—and how much I'd like to see much more of you?'

Mind: The job?
Heart: He gave it to you.
Mind: The car?
Heart: He arranged it.
Mind: And Sue 'Tell it like it is' Bailey?
Heart: He created you.
Mind: And what is left?
Heart: Me.

Susan Bailey stood up, threw her napkin onto the table and began to walk to the door. She turned and smiled graciously, 'I'm suddenly not very hungry, Mr Kingston. Please give my best wishes to your wife.'

Cecil Kingston would never know just how sickening she found him, nor how much damage that disastrous lunchtime meeting had done.

7
A Sense of Loss

The office was silent. It was seven o'clock in the evening. Sue had turned out the overhead fluorescent lighting and was working in the dim glow of her desk lamp. She had resigned from the sports centre and avoided, where she could, all contact with Steve Willshaw and his so-called 'Board'. She was often missing from her desk during the day but put in the hours at night.

The letter before her was from a young widow whose life had been torn apart by the loss of her husband. Sue struggled to remember what bereavement felt like, for even as an eight year old, she had known the anguish of grief. She'd distanced herself from many of the memories, but there were times, like tonight, when she could still feel her father close to her.

When you lose someone you have loved you begin a journey through many painful stages of human experience. There is a phase of 'disbelief', a stage when you feel numb, and when you can't come to terms with what's happened. During this phase you may weep without cause when you hear a song on the radio or discover an old letter from your loved one.

Grief isn't resolved suddenly, but usually diminishes

gradually over the years. From time to time, even as I write, my feelings of loss for my father flare up without warning.

Sue's mind back-tracked down the years and she felt again what it was like at home after her dad died. Half remembered conversations, the sound of her mother's sobbing, and a gnawing sense of loss which had robbed her of her childhood security. The grief had deeply scarred her, and much of her childhood had been taken up with coming to terms with it.

In my life the loss of someone I love has always led to unavoidable suffering and feelings so intense that I've sometimes felt I'm going insane. Dreams have been important, though often disturbing. I've woken in the midst of nightmares involving my loved one, and have been engulfed by waves of sadness. I guess that's how my mind comes to terms with things the way they are.

All of us have to learn how to die with the dead, in order to live with the living. Grief, for me, has been an attempt to deal with the parts of my life that are over, but still precious.

She sat back in her chair and read what she'd written on her screen. Sue wondered if she was right to reveal so much of herself in what she wrote. Not for the first time, she began to feel very vulnerable. Suddenly her concentration was broken by the sound of the vacuum.

She continued to work, but her heart sank when the door opened and the loud drone of the vacuum grew nearer. At last she looked up, unable to ignore Elsie any longer.

'Hi there, Elsie. How's things?' Sue struggled to sound friendly.

'Fine, Sue, fine.' Elsie said, barely audible above the sound of the vacuum. She didn't even pause to look up.

Sue went back to her article on grief but couldn't concentrate. Elsie's back was turned to her. She watched as the older woman unplugged the cleaner and pulled it clumsily out of the room behind her.

Sue felt guilty. She knew that she owed Elsie an apology, but she'd never been good at saying sorry at the best of times. She got up and followed Elsie into the hallway.

'Look, I'm sorry Elsie, but your problem just wasn't the kind of thing that I could tackle through the column . . . and I've been swamped by other questions. Okay?'

Elsie continued to pull the vacuum, looking away. She didn't reply.

Sue edged round to look at Elsie's face, determined to establish eye contact, but when she did so she gasped. Elsie's right eye was bloodshot and swollen, and the swelling extended from her eyebrow to her cheek.

'What happened to you, Elsie? When did you get this?'

Elsie turned away, still silent.

'But how?

As Elsie pulled the vacuum across the hall Sue heard her mutter, 'Just leave it, Sue. Just leave it, okay?'

Sue felt that Elsie had a lot more to tell. 'If I can do anything, all you have to do is ask, okay?' Sue knew she sounded patronising again.

Elsie turned, 'I asked you before, remember?' She pushed the vacuum back toward the cleaner's room, 'It's too late now anyway. I've got to get out.' She closed the door behind her.

Sue returned to her desk and gazed at her screen. She struggled to concentrate, but her mind wouldn't rest. At last she dialled Pete's number, a number indelibly engraved on her memory.

'Pete? It's Sue,' she said, trembling with fear.

'Hello . . .'

There was a long silence, as if neither knew what to say next. Sue took a deep breath. 'I need your help, Pete.'

'Okay.' He sounded warm and friendly.

'I'm doing this agony column . . .'

'I've seen it. Very impressive.' His praise somehow sounded hollow.

'Do you know much about evictions?'

'Enough to get by. I've handled a few in my time. Usually on the part of householders, mind.'

'Someone I know is being evicted soon. What's the procedure?'

'It's a real hassle for the landlord.' His manner changed—it was as if he had put on his professional mask. 'It demands a court appearance, evidence of reason for eviction, and usually a time delay. If there's any possibility of the tenant being given a stay of execution, so to speak, the court often opts for that. Especially if there are children involved.'

'If I sent you a few details, would you look into it for me—for old time's sake?'

'Fine. No problem.' There was a long pause. 'I still love you Sue.'

'I need to leave the romantic side out of things right now. I can't handle it. Okay?'

There was a long pause. 'I can't let go. Tell me, Ms tell it like it is, how do I deal with that?'

He hung up and she heard the dull sound of the dialling tone. Sue turned back to her screen, and struggled to find space in her thoughts to concentrate again, but she couldn't.

Mind: What have you done to him?
Heart: Hurt him, I guess.
Mind: And how did you hurt him?
Heart: I pretended that I loved him.
Mind: And why did you pretend?
Heart: Because I didn't want to hurt him.
Mind: And now that he knows?
Heart: The pain is greater.
Mind: And why is that?
Heart: Because he feels betrayed.

Pete was dealing with an acute sense of loss. It had been so much harder for Pete than she'd imagined. But it hadn't been easy for her, either. She still mourned him and often remembered the good times they'd shared. Life had moved on, but still she missed him. She turned to her keyboard, closed the file on grief, and opened another on loss.

My perception of myself was bound up with my partner, and when the relationship ended it affected the way that I saw myself. It cut at the very core of my being.

Even relationships which have gone through years of tension can trigger enormous emotional trauma when they end. In a recent study researchers discovered that even among those partners who initiated the separation the experience was far more devastating than they had imagined. That, certainly, was borne out in my own experience.

Many lovers lose their sense of reality after they separate, a state that sociologists call 'anomie'. Others find it impossible to end a relationship emotionally and persist in hope and commitment for several years.

Bertrand Russell wrote: 'One cannot transfer love to another person as if it were a piece of luggage to be taken from one train to another.' When you have loved you must pass through the pain of grief and separation, and I, for one, have found no short-cuts to happiness.

The door opened again. A shaft of light from the hallway lit the news-room. 'I'm off now. I'll leave the lockin' to you,' Elsie drawled half-heartedly.

Sue turned to face her and saw again Elsie's swollen cheek and bloodshot eye. 'No Elsie, I'm leaving now. I'll give you a lift.'

The night was dark, and there was a damp drizzle in the air. The two women drove in silence, but the chatter of the car radio covered their awkwardness. When at last Sue had negotiated the narrow road and found a parking space Elsie clambered out and muttered 'Thanks'. She was evidently depressed.

Sue attempted a three point turn, which in such a narrow space took more like fifteen. As she completed the manoeuvre and was about to drive away Sue noticed two men approach Elsie's door. She gently braked and reversed back into the parking space. She turned off the lights and watched.

One of the men opened Elsie's door with a key and they both disappeared inside. Sue turned off the ignition, and the chatter of the radio ceased. She felt disturbed. She wound down the window and listened to the noise of the city. She felt the specks of damp drizzle falling on her cheek.

About five minutes later the front door opened again and one of the men emerged carrying the front of the large sofa covered in red silk. He almost tripped over the front step and the other man cursed him loudly. They carried the sofa to a white high topped van and pushed it into the open tailgate. They went back inside. A few minutes later one of them returned with a television set and the other followed with an upright chair.

Shortly after they had disappeared inside again Sue followed them in through the open door and ran up the stairs. When she entered the lounge she saw Elsie facing the window.

'What's the problem?' Sue said, in her most authoritative sounding tone.

'Who are you, madam?' asked the older of the two, a man in his early forties with a large paunch which rippled over his wide leather belt.

'I'm a reporter at the *Courier* and I have an interest in this situation.'

'Don't bother us lady. We're just moving this stuff over to the bed and breakfast. It's what you want—ain't it?' He looked accusingly at Elsie.

'Do you have an eviction order?' Sue demanded.

'They don't need one!' Elsie snapped, 'I'm going because I ain't got no choice.'

'Mam . . .' whined the little boy. He was sat on the floor, and he was clutching the end of her skirt for security.

'Shut it or you'll get it . . . right son?' The boy looked pleadingly up at her. He was sullen.

Sue felt awkward because Elsie didn't seem to want her there, and besides, she felt powerless to do anything. She placed a hand on Elsie's shoulder, 'Call me tomorrow at work. Okay?'

Elsie nodded, but said nothing. The two men continued to strip the house. They were evidently not bothered about Elsie's furniture. Things were taken down to the van as they were, without any attempt to cushion or protect them. Sue followed as they struggled clumsily down the narrow staircase with a sideboard. There was a loud crash and its glass door shattered. The younger man cursed loudly again because the glass had cut his finger.

Sue followed them into the street and watched them struggling towards the white van; it had the letters ADCA painted on the door. Sue got into her car and started the ignition.

Mind: Running away are you?
Heart: Maybe.
Mind: Couldn't you have stayed awhile?
Heart: I'm not sure that I could handle it.
Mind: Are you at the limits of your caring?
Heart: Maybe I don't care at all.

Sue drove back to Paula's feeling more of a failure than ever. She opened the door and dropped her leather case with a thud. She could hear muffled voices and wondered if she might meet the legendary Brian. Suddenly the lounge door opened and Pete was standing there.

'Oh . . . it's you. I was just going.' He was flushed with embarrassment. 'I just brought some papers round for you . . . about eviction.' He pressed them into her hand.

Sue looked into his soft eyes and realised how much she'd missed him. 'Thanks, Pete.'

'Look, about everything . . . can't we still meet. Can't we still be friends?'

'I'm not sure I can handle it, Pete. It's still too soon.' She was struggling to keep control.

'You seem so distant.'

'It's just too painful for me to be real with you yet.' She looked down in embarrassment.

'Do you still love me?'

Sue took a deep breath. Her voice became harsh and unsympathetic. 'I just can't handle it . . . all right? Please leave me alone. The time will come when we can talk. But it's not yet. Okay?'

'Well, thanks for nothing.' His voice had become harsher too, 'You've totally ruined my life, Susan Bailey, you gave me a hope and a dream—something to live for—and now you've taken it away. You'll never know how you've destroyed me nor how much it's hurt. Don't you understand? Can't you even begin to imagine what you've done to me?'

She opened the door for him and stood, her head leaning against it, as if ushering him out. Pete brushed past her. 'Pete . . .' she whispered. But he was gone. She looked down at the papers in her hand. They were too late to help Elsie.

Paula emerged from the lounge looking embarrassed. 'I'm sorry, Sue, I didn't mean to let him in. It looks like you could do with a big mug of hot chocolate.'

'Please Paula, don't let him come again, promise?'

'Anything you say, boss. Anyway, where've you been? It's late.'

Sue didn't sleep well. Pete's words rolled round and round her brain, she hadn't realised how much she'd hurt him nor quite how much he'd cared.

She felt very tired the following morning and decided not to hurry in to work. It was after lunch by the time she parked the Toyota in the staff car park, but she still couldn't face going in. She turned and walked back down the service road toward the canal.

She was exhausted, and walked slowly beside the grey water feeling very depressed. As she emerged from the darkness of the bridge she looked into Father Thomas's eyes. It was as though he had been sitting on the green bench and waiting for her. Sue slumped onto the bench with Father Thomas beside her and he looked into her red eyes. She sighed, 'Is the confessional open for business?'

Father Thomas smiled, 'Of course.'

And then she turned to him and said, 'I don't really give a damn, you know.'

An hour later, Sue Bailey walked back toward 'The Box' with a new lightness in her step.

On the towpath beyond the bridge she saw Budd walking quickly towards her. He seemed preoccupied and distant. He didn't acknowledge her or return her smile. Sue continued on towards the *Courier,* and wondered where Budd was going in such a hurry.

Budd walked quickly, striding toward the bend in the canal like a man hurrying to fulfil an appointment. He opened the black metal gate and clanked it closed behind him, and then he stopped, as if to compose himself. His eyes were fixed on the gravestone in front of him.

Maria Hampton.
Born: 1969
Died: 1991
He will wipe the tears from their eyes.

Budd walked slowly to the grave and sank to his knees on the wet earth beside it. He snatched the bunch of dead flowers from the pot and threw them to one side. And he wept. He wept for Maria Hampton.

As he wept he felt an arm placed around his shoulder, and he knew that the one beside him was weeping, too. Father Thomas grasped him to himself and felt the anguish in the sobbing of the young man he knew so well. They remained there, weeping, for some considerable time.

At long last, when the weeping was ended and the tears had been dried Father Thomas helped Budd to his feet, and the two men walked slowly back towards the old black gate. Father Thomas and Budd walked the canal path from the church gate to the bridge and back, and, because their conversation was far from complete, they turned and walked the route again.

Budd had walked this path with Father Thomas before, and found that he could share more deeply when they walked together like this. He'd known Father Thomas for more than five years and saw him as a friend as well as a priest.

Maria Hampton, the girl he'd loved throughout his teenage years, had died three months before the wedding. The youth group camping holiday in Southern Italy had ended in tragedy when Maria had suffered an asthma attack one hot and airless night.

He had carried her out of the tent and into the open field to give her air, while others ran to get an ambulance. He held her in his arms and watched her helplessly as she gasped for breath. She seemed to struggle to cling to life itself. And tears poured from her eyes and ran down her cheeks in long streams. As Budd had kissed her tears away he tasted the helplessness of her struggle. It had been the most painful experience of his life and it had scarred him in ways beyond his understanding.

'Are you ready . . . at last?' Father Thomas whispered as they approached the bridge for the second time.

'Maybe.' Budd's eyes were fixed on the path ahead.

'I've told you before, you can only let go when you've had time to grieve . . . and, God knows . . . you've grieved for Maria for long enough.' Father Thomas threw a pebble into the stillness of the grey water. The tall black clouds of dusk were approaching.

Budd glanced at Father Thomas again, and, for just

an instant, their eyes met; and the priest knew for sure that Budd was ready. Father Thomas smiled a wry smile. 'The older I get, the more convinced I become that things have a wonderful way of turning out all right in the end.' Both men knew that the conversation was over, and the healing complete. They went their separate ways. Father Thomas turned back towards the lock, and Budd continued on towards 'The Box'.

8

Dark Days

'One thing's for sure, if you start to feel a failure it will affect everything you do! Somehow you have to climb out of this spiral of negativism and start to think differently about the future.' Sue was struggling to concentrate. She was approaching the deadline on her column and the reply to the question about failure was proving difficult.

'First of all, look at your situation calmly and coldly, and stick to facts rather than opinions. Look rationally at your failure, leaving out your emotions and feelings, and begin to look at it in a different way.' There was a loud buzz of conversation in the news-room, and Jonathan's voice was particularly irritating. He was telling Budd a crude joke at his desk immediately behind hers. He really irritated her.

'If you haven't done your job as well as you could have done and feel you've failed, you should regard it as a learning experience rather than a personal disaster.'

She turned to Jonathan. 'Will you shut up? I just can't concentrate.'

'Listen to little Miss Agony,' he sneered 'Got a bit of a problem today, have we?'

'Look, I'm up to copy deadline—I need to think.'

Jonathan smirked, 'You surely don't need to use your brain to write that stuff, do you?'

Budd placed his hand on Jonathan's shoulder. 'Leave it, Jono, leave it.'

Sue's phone buzzed and she picked up the receiver. It was Elsie. Jonathan returned to his joke.

'Sue, is that you?'

'Yes, of course, Elsie, how's things?'

'Bad Sue, bad. I didn't know how terrible this place was.' She sounded distressed.

'Is there enough room?'

Elsie sighed. 'You must be kidding. All three of us are in a tiny room. They've had to put the furniture in store. We can't even cook. And it's damp. I think there's problems with the roof. I can't keep the kids here . . .' Elsie's voice began to break up with emotion.

Mind: Why not run away?
Heart: I can't.
Mind: It's not your problem.
Heart: Yes it is.
Mind: But do you really care?
Heart: From here on in I do.

'Hang on in there Elsie. I'll see what I can do.' Sue jotted down the address of the Bourne Hotel in her notebook. She glanced at her watch—she had ten minutes to deadline.

I'm learning that there's no point in worrying about falling short of a goal. Life's too short for that! And I've decided to stop wallowing in self blame.

I'm going to start being my own defence lawyer and to stop living under the shadow of past mistakes. The future begins now!

Sue smiled in satisfaction and programmed the piece to go across to paste up. Budd and Jonathan were still talking at the desk behind hers. They were looking at Budd's pictures from the local soccer match. Jonathan was looking for a photo to illustrate his piece about some pathetic player.

'Are you busy Budd?' Sue interrupted.

Budd turned and smiled. 'No, not really, why?'

'I think I've got a job for you.'

Jonathan dropped the pile of pictures onto his desk. 'More posey photos of Ms "Tell it like it is" I expect.'

Budd turned and smiled. 'Jealous of all my attention are you, Jono?'

Sue left the room with Budd trailing behind her. 'Hang on a mo—I'll get my camera bag,' but she was already on her way out to the car.

Sue and Budd met heavy traffic on their way to the Bourne Hotel, which was in an area which had deteriorated rapidly under the threat of redevelopment.

'What's the score?' Budd was intrigued.

'I want to do a piece about the way that Elsie's been treated. I can smell plenty of dirt around this story.'

'But what's that to do with your column?'

'Nothing, Budd. It's nothing to do with the column but I've got to write it for my own sanity.'

'And?' he turned to face her. The car window was open, and her long fair hair was blowing free. He watched her with pleasure.

'I can't run away from Elsie's problems. It's time I did something constructive for once. I need to right a few wrongs—make my work count for something.'

'Does Steve Willshaw know?'

'He will, soon enough.'

The Bourne Hotel, like the area in which it was situated, had seen better days. Once its Edwardian frontage had been the entrance to a world of elegant splendour, but now the grey walls were peeling. The large black front door exhibited a large white swastika, painted by local skinheads. The window curtains were drab and faded and the window boxes untended and overgrown. Sue pulled into the concrete area in front of the hotel. It had once been an ornate garden.

Elsie's room was even more squalid than Sue had imagined. The three beds filled much of the floor space, packing cases were stacked to the ceiling on one side of the room, and there were piles of clothes on the bed because there was nowhere to store anything. A two ringed electric cooker was standing on a rickety table, its flex split and scorched. The room smelt damp, and a dark stain on the wall indicated a serious roofing problem.

Elsie sighed. 'Thank God you've come, Sue.' She was wearing the same pink bathrobe—though it was noticeably dirtier than before. She looked dishevelled, and she was barefoot. Her cheek was swollen and her right eye was still bloodshot. She had evidently been crying. The two children were sitting on the floor in the corner of the room with their faces close to a television screen. They were watching cartoons and the bright colours glared in the darkness of the room.

'This is terrible, Elsie. It's just not acceptable.' Sue whispered.

Elsie sat down on the bed, 'There's nothing no one can do. It's all my own fault.' Tears were welling up in her eyes.

Sue sat down and placed her arm gently round the older woman. 'I'd like to tell the world about this, Elsie, and then I'm sure something will be done.'

Budd was already busy. He was taking pictures of Sue beside Elsie, of the squat room, and photos of the two children in front of the tea-chests.

'Are you sure these pictures won't cause trouble?' Elsie pleaded, but she spoke as someone who was powerless over her own destiny.

Sue assured her that she'd take care of everything, and once she felt at ease, Elsie began to describe all that had happened since arriving at the hotel. Sue scribbled in her notebook; and she felt a surge of anger growing within her. At last, when the story was told and the notebook closed, Sue dug into her pocket and gave Elsie a twenty pound note.

'Take the kids out for something to eat.'

Sue and Budd drove back to the office in silence. When they arrived Budd simply said, 'I'll have these on your desk within two hours,' and left for the darkroom.

Sue sat back down at her desk and looked into her blank blue screen and saw Elsie, sitting on the bed, with tears in her eyes. The anger rose within her again. She knew that after ten years of writing what the *Courier* wanted that it was time she wrote something for herself. The anger she felt about Elsie startled her and through it she discovered a power in her words that she'd never known before.

The angry words poured onto the screen. This wasn't her usual style, it was pithy and hard-hitting and headlined 'Scandal at the Bourne'. Sue described the tactics of ADCA, the needs of the kids, and the squalor at the hotel. And as she wrote she felt inspired and was carried along by a wave of truth that exhilarated her.

She dialled Steve's number. 'I've got an extra piece this week, Steve—it's for one of the general news pages. It could even make the leader. It's on my screen if you'd like to read it.'

Steve sighed. 'I've already read it. You'd better come up, Sue. Right now.'

The line went dead.

She snatched her notebook and climbed the stairs to Steve's office and gently closed the door behind her. He was sitting at his desk and staring into his screen.

'What the hell are you playing at?' He looked up at her. His eyebrows were furrowed. 'Who gave you permission to go nosing around at the Bourne?'

She pulled the chair closer to his desk and sat down. 'What's wrong? I thought the piece had bite.'

'You're an agony aunt, not some politico agitator.' He loosened the knot on his old school tie. 'You were well out of line going down there. Why didn't you clear it with me first, like you're supposed to?'

'I've worked here for ten years, Steve—I know a good

story when I see one.' Sue was struggling to hold her temper. 'How dare you try to tell me my job?'

'Well, join the club,' Steve sneered. 'We all have to do what we're told—me included.'

'Well I've had enough of it. I'm a journalist—and I'm going to start writing like one.' She leant forward, as if in earnest.

'Well you can damn well go and write some place else, because I don't want it in my paper. I've got enough problems as it is.'

'I couldn't care less about your problems, Steve. This is an important piece and I'm not going to let it go . . . not this one.' She sounded hard and uncompromising.

Steve took a swig of coffee and frowned. It was cold. He was wrestling to gain some equilibrium because he was near to losing his temper completely. He took a deep breath.

'For God's sake, Sue, have you gone completely insane? Have you any idea what you're asking of me?'

'Oh yes, Steve, I understand the consequences, all right. If you print this piece a woman and her kids might get somewhere decent to live . . . and some bent debt collection agency might stop beating people up . . . and the Bourne Hotel might get condemned as uninhabitable.'

'The article is spiked. It won't appear. You'd better get used to the idea. And that's final.' He was furious.

Susan Bailey glared at him in anger. 'Either that article appears in the *Courier* this week or I'm out for good. Understand?'

Steven Willshaw stood up and walked slowly round to the front of his desk and leant against it. He towered above her.

'Now just you listen to me, Ms Bailey, and listen well. If it wasn't for me you'd have been out of a job by now. Let me put it as plainly as I can—you've upset the Board, and the Board wants your column out. Understand?'

Sue felt as if she was going to faint. She took a deep

breath and looked up at Steve. 'Well I guess that's it then, Steve. I couldn't carry on here, anyway.'

She slowly got up and walked to the door. She felt he wanted to say something more, but he didn't. She closed the door behind her. Her ten years at the *Courier* were over.

The day was overcast and cool, but by the time Sue arrived at Father Thomas's vicarage she felt very hot. She'd walked quickly in order to distance herself from the events of the day, but it hadn't worked. A dark feeling of hopelessness wrapped around her like a cloak.

She knocked repeatedly on the vicarage door, but there was no reply. She scribbled a few lines in her notebook asking Father Thomas to call her at home, tore the sheet out, and dropped it through the letterbox.

She turned to go, but, inquisitive as ever, she peeked in the study window. The room was bare. Father Thomas had evidently been busy since she'd last seen him piling books into his car. The empty house seemed strange.

The News-room was practically empty by the time she got back because many of the team had gone off to a local pub for lunch together. Sue dropped her brown case on her desk, and noticed that her screen was still lit and the words of the fateful 'Bourne' article still displayed. She printed off a hard copy, pulled off the paper, and strolled leisurely up to Budd's darkroom. The darkroom 'Engaged' light was illuminated, so she knocked gently.

'How long, Budd? It's Sue.' There was urgency in her voice.

'I'm just about finished . . . these pics of the hotel really tell the story. Best stuff I've done in ages.'

She heard the door lock click and the door opened. Budd was grinning at her. 'Come and look at these.'

He moved the pictures around in the fixer, each one illuminated only by the dull red darkroom light. They were shadowy and moody—classic photojournalism style—and so different from Budd's normal material.

'It's a pity they'll never be used.'

'You what?' Budd turned from the sink where he'd been washing his hands. He picked up an old towel.

'The story's spiked. There's no way he'll use it.'

'And what does that mean?' Budd's voice was soft and sympathetic.

'It means that I'm out. I'm through with the *Courier*, Budd. I've got to be me—and I've quit.' Her voice was full of emotion.

He held open his arms and she stepped into them, but, almost as soon as he had gently closed his arms around her she pushed him away. He turned back to the sink in embarrassment

'By the way,' she said, as if nothing had happened, 'I brought you a copy of the Bourne piece I wrote, just for posterity.' She took the paper out of her dress pocket and unfolded it carefully. She was about to place it next to the bowl of fixer.

'Not there . . . it'll get ruined . . . put it on my desk over there.' Budd muttered.

She put the paper down on his desk, and as she did so she saw something which made her heart thump with panic. On the desk was a blue envelope marked with the words . . . 'The *Courier*, Box 104296.'

She picked up the envelope, her mind was reeling, and she swung round to face him.

'You must be sick, Budd. How could you? Conning me like this. Knowing . . . all the time.' Her eyes blazed with anger.

Budd was wiping his hands on the towel. 'What on earth do you . . .?'

She tore the envelope in two and threw it back onto the desk and ran down to the News-room. She felt sick. The News-room was full again. They'd all returned from lunch and Jonathan was sat on his desk holding forth as usual.

'. . . I told you all along it was a stupid idea. Sue Bailey can't sort out her own life, so how can she possibly sort out . . .'

'Shut your stupid face . . .' she yelled.

He swung round toward her, his blotchy face flushing with anger. 'What's your problem, lady? Like to "Tell it like it is" to uncle Jonathan?' He grabbed her hand and stroked it with the other.

'Take your dirty hands off of me.' The work stopped all over the office and there was silence. She wrenched herself free.

Sue snatched up her brown case from the desk and stormed out of the double doors. She drove the Toyota out of the car park at full-speed, the tyres squealing as she cornered into the road. It had been one hell of a day.

Budd slumped into his chair. He, too, was starting to feel sick. He looked up at the line of black and white pictures of the Bourne pegged up to dry, and back at the torn blue envelope in front of him. For him, too, it had been one hell of a day.

Sue was driving in a dream toward Pete's house. She didn't really know why, because she knew he'd be at work, and anyway, she didn't really belong there any more. She sat outside the house she'd once called 'home' and wondered what to do. Tears were rolling down her cheeks.

She looked at her watch and realised that Pete wouldn't be home for two hours. She locked the car and strolled off across the common between the big trees she knew so well.

As she walked she felt weighed down by the different situations in her life. Her mind was full of images, and voices and she felt powerless to change anything. The column. The 'Board'. Her feelings for Pete. Budd. Elsie's problems. The bust-up with Steve. The loss of her job. She desperately wanted to run away but there seemed nowhere to run.

At the far side of the common there was a pub which

was open all hours so she went in and drank a glass of red wine, and then two more. The music of love songs filled the empty bar.

It was dark by the time that Sue got back to her car, and she was relieved to see that Pete's lounge light was on. The yellow wallpaper she'd chosen looked welcoming through the darkness. She still had the front door key on her keyring, and only just resisted the temptation to use it. She rang the doorbell. Pete opened the door and welcomed her in. He made her coffee, and tried to be as civil as he could, but he was still hurting from their last meeting, and he was in no mood to be rebuffed again.

'I've had one hell of a day,' she moaned, looking for sympathy. But there was none.

'Really?' He sounded disinterested.

'I've lost my job over that eviction story.'

His expression didn't change. 'You always did like to live on the edge.' He was measuring every word.

She looked at him intensely. 'Pete, did you really love me?'

'That's all rather academic now, don't you think? The way you've treated me this last few weeks after . . . after such a good time. Well, I guess I'm hurt, that's all.'

'But did you love me? Really?'

'I think you're one hell of a messed up young woman, if you really want to know. I don't know why . . . I did my best. Any normal two people who've shared what we've shared would be planning a life together . . . kids . . . the whole thing. But you were never satisfied . . . about anything.' He took another swig of coffee.

'It was all right for a time.'

'Yes, but I did everything to please you. I did everything to make you happy . . . but you never understood . . . you never recognised it. And then . . . after all that . . . you just walked out.'

Pete got up and looked out of the window at the dark shapes of the trees on the common opposite. He was fighting to retain control. 'You've used me, Sue, from start to finish you've used me—and, if that wasn't enough, you had to use our relationship as copy for that damn column of yours.'

He swung round to face her.

'You don't know who you are, Sue. You'll never settle . . . to anything . . . or with anyone . . . until you get that sorted. You're just a lost soul, Susan Bailey, and I don't know how to help you any more.'

Sue got up and opened the lounge door without speaking, and as she did so she caught a glimpse of a tall brunette disappearing into the bedroom opposite. She had been listening at the door.

Sue slammed the front door as she left. It was a final statement—the closing of another chapter of her life.

Budd's darkroom was a place of security for him. He felt like a king in this place of black walls and strange red shadows. He sat at his desk, pencil in hand, and stared up at the mirror in front of him. He took up the leather-bound drawing book and grappled with the self-portrait he'd attempted so many times before. He was struggling with the eyes again, he never seemed to get them right. Drawing was his way of thinking things through.

Sue's journey back to Paula's was long and depressing. The city traffic was at a standstill and she sat at the wheel staring at the swirling wipers and the maze of headlights beyond. The scenes of her life played out before her, and the rhythmic turning of the wipers seemed to accentuate the despair she felt.

Mind: What are you looking for, Susan Bailey?
Heart: I'm looking for love.
Mind: And wasn't Pete's love enough?
Heart: No . . . there is a greater love . . . but I cannot find it.
Mind: Is there nowhere else to look?
Heart: No. Nowhere else.

At last she reached the accident which had caused the jam and saw the torch of flame leaping from the car and lighting up the night sky. Glass had shattered everywhere. A horn was blaring. A dark plume of smoke was rising from the burning wreck. And everywhere there were shrill excited voices—a maze of headlights—and a crowd of onlookers standing by the roadside.

A girl draped in a blanket was sitting on the kerb and crying hysterically. A thin stream of blood was trickling down her cheek. The girl looked like Sue. Somewhere, in the distance, she heard the sound of a siren.

Sue pulled up outside the corner store and went inside. She had finally decided. When she got back to the flat she went straight to her room and sank onto the bed. Her head throbbed with pain, and it was as if her whole being ached.

The bedroom door opened . . . 'Guess what . . .?' Paula's voice sounded shrill. Sue made no reply, but looked at the silhouette in the doorway and smelt the sweet perfume.

'It's Brian. Things are looking up. He called me today . . .' Paula giggled. 'Wish me luck.'

Sue didn't respond, but turned over in the bed and listened as Paula opened the front door and banged it shut behind her. This was one time when she needed someone with her. She had never felt so alone in her life.

Mind: You've really screwed up, haven't you?
Heart: Yes.
Mind: And what Pete said . . . was it right?
Heart: Yes. It was right.
Mind: And are you lost . . .?
Heart: I'll never find my way again . . .
Mind: And what will stop the pain?
Heart: Death . . . I guess.
Mind: And what after death?

Heart: Oblivion. Bliss. The end of struggle. No more screwing up.
Mind: And what if there is a way ahead?
Heart: And what if there is not . . .?

She took up her diary and scanned its pages. Ever since childhood Sue Bailey had used words to find the way ahead. Childish words at first. Words about her father's death, written out, because her intensity of feeling had to be dealt with somehow. Sometimes the words were poems, and sometimes they just told the story of her days, but there were always words, because this was how Susan Bailey came to terms with life. It seemed ironic that she was using words to chart her final choice, the end of life itself.

> 'I guess that no one will understand why I've done what I've done because no one really knows my agony. It's not the unhappiness, I could handle that. It's the overwhelming sense of futility that I can take no more. I face a wall of burning questions about my life, my existence, and my future . . . and it seems there is no way through.

Sue placed her diary on the bedside table. She took two containers of pills and a whisky bottle from her bag. She poured a tall glass, and drank deep. Her throat burned. The pills tasted powdery and dry. She poured another glass and drank again until, at last, the bottle was empty and the tablets gone. And slowly she drifted into a dark and heavy dream . . .

Paula's date with Brian was a disaster from start to finish. She'd waited for him outside the pub for thirty minutes until her hands were blue with cold. When he did arrive he made no apology. He never did.

Brian was a man of dark moods, and Paula never quite knew how to take him. They sat in silence at a table near the bar. Her every attempt at conversation was rebuffed by a 'yes' or 'no' response. There was no joy in their being together, no anticipation, no affection. She suspected that he'd rather be with someone else.

After her third drink Paula considered her options as she'd considered them so many times before. Perhaps, at last, it was time to take Sue's advice and to end this futile relationship once and for all.

She tried to look him in the eyes, but he evaded her. She cleared her throat and whispered, 'I think it's time we finished.' He looked relieved, and she slowly got up to go.

'Yes. I reckon so.' His eyes still evaded hers. He was looking toward the bar, and a pretty girl who was sitting on her own.

Paula made her way home feeling very low. She slammed the front door behind her and strode to the kitchen to boil some milk. It was a bitter night and she was frozen to the core. She made two mugs of chocolate and crept into Sue's room hoping for a little understanding. She turned on the bedroom light and stood transfixed.

Sue's face was ashen grey, and her lips were blue.

9
Life and Death

Sue lay in the misty shadowland between life and death, her mind drifting somewhere between reality and fantasy. She watched the familiar faces floating past her field of view. She couldn't actively form logical patterns of thought, but the questions which had driven her to this place of shadows still echoed somewhere in the caverns of her mind.

Mind: Who are you?
Heart: . . .
Mind: Do you care?
Heart: . . .
Mind: What is love?
Heart: . . .
Mind: Where is life?

Sue Bailey looked like a corpse in the stark white lights of the crash room. Somewhere a young nurse dropped a silver bowl of instruments which clattered to the floor. Someone cursed. A second doctor ran in, pulling plastic gloves over his hands. There was urgency in their voices. But she was aware of no pain.

'It's the usual,' said the younger doctor to the consultant, who had just arrived.

'Respiratory depression, convulsions, hypertension, arrhythmias—she's OD'd on anti-depressants.'

An alarm sounded—not loud, but disturbing. The consultant swung round to his patient.

He looked at the irregular line on the screen. 'Defibrillate—now.'

There was a veneer of professionalism in all they were doing, but it only thinly covered the raw nervous energy of fighting death on the front line.

Standing behind the medical team in their pristine white uniforms there was another figure. Motionless, statue-like, his face white against his jet black suit. Father Thomas stood staring at Sue, struggling to pray and to find words fitting for so grave a situation. He'd been summoned by the hospital receptionist at Paula's request and had come immediately.

Outside, in the waiting room, Paula was standing looking out of the window at the tall bare trees bathed in the orange glow of the neon street lights. Her ginger hair and freckled face were reflected in the window, and she too stood motionless, willing Sue to live. Her mind still echoed with the memory of the date with Brian which had ended so suddenly less than an hour before. She realised again what a failure the relationship had been, and felt overwhelmed by despair.

She thought of Sue and wondered, if Sue should die, how she would survive. Her own life seemed to have been dogged by short-term relationships, and she'd hoped for something more lasting in her friendship with Sue.

Paula recognised, too, that her early return from the disastrous date with Brian had probably saved Sue's life. She wished she hadn't gone out at all. Why had she been so full of her own plans that she hadn't noticed Sue's need? Why was it that she managed to screw up every time?

The following morning Steve Willshaw sat at Sue's desk and typed hurriedly into her keyboard. There was a dark, sombre atmosphere in the News-room, and although business continued as usual there was a hushed reverence which pervaded every conversation. News of Sue's attempted suicide had travelled fast around the *Courier*, and everyone found it difficult to comprehend. Sue had been popular among the people at 'The Box' and no one really knew what to say. She would be missed.

The deadline for the next edition had already passed. But the team at paste-up had held Sue's page over to be printed last. They'd withdrawn her copy and replaced it with a large photo of Sue and a stock feature on EuroDisney to fill up the space. All that remained was Steve's brief statement, but he couldn't seem to find the words. He knew that what he wrote would be read and analysed by *Courier* readers everywhere.

He'd already tried to write the piece at the screen in his own office, but couldn't find the words. By sitting at Sue's desk and using her keyboard he figured that he could get a little closer to the sentiment he was searching for.

Late on Tuesday night Sue Bailey was admitted to the General where her condition is described as 'critical'. Sue, whose weekly agony column has become a firm favourite with thousands of our readers, has attempted suicide. Her agony column is quite irreplaceable, so, instead of continuing with it, we will be re-starting our popular 'Local Faces' feature.

He pressed the computer keys and programmed the terminal to send the material to paste-up. He didn't feel comfortable about what he'd written, but there was no point in trying to explain anything more. Steve got up from Sue's swivel chair and turned to Jonathan who was seated at the desk behind.

'It's all yours now, Jono. Put Sue's stuff into a cardboard box and drop it by my office. I'll get it delivered to her house. The quicker you can get this new page established the better. I'm looking for full copy for next week's edition within forty-eight hours.'

'No problem,' Jonathan smiled. He'd already piled the contents of his own desk into two cardboard boxes, and was clearing the last few things away. For him it was like a dream come true. He'd worked for the *Courier* since leaving school at eighteen when he'd begun by covering the little league football matches and the darts tournaments. He'd resented Sue's arrival from the start, and her college education had meant that her career had advanced more quickly than his own. He'd always wanted to write a column for the paper, and had longed for the opportunity to move beyond the world of sport.

When Steve returned to his office one floor above, Budd was leaning against the wall, waiting for him. He had been there for quite some time. Budd was like a gentle giant. Well over six feet in height, but very lean and sallow skinned.

'Five minutes, Steve?' Budd demanded.

'Okay, if it's crucial.' Steve opened the door and slumped into the chair behind his desk.

Budd remained standing, though Steve had motioned for him to sit down. 'I'm sorry you didn't use Sue's piece about the Bourne.'

'Well that's the papers . . . better luck next week.' He sounded sarcastic.

'I'm sorry for you, Steve.'

'And why is that?'

Budd dug his hands into his pockets and sighed. 'Sue Bailey's the best damn reporter this paper's ever had. She really cared. If this paper was really interested in the truth you'd have run her stuff. It was the least you could have done.' There was an emotion in his voice which irritated Steve. No one really understood the pressure he'd been under.

'True or false . . . I don't know, and I don't much care. If we'd run that stuff all hell would have broken loose, and it just wasn't worth the hassle. This is the *North London Courier*, Budd . . . not the *Sunday Times*. People read us for the TV listings and the small ads . . . not for grand exposées of corruption in high places. If Sue wanted to write that kind of stuff she should have taken some different career decisions.'

Budd frowned. 'Is there no chance you'll take her back?'

Steve leant back in his chair and placed his hands behind his head. 'Not in a million years, my friend. No way.'

There was a knock at the door, but before Steve could shout 'Wait', it opened. Jonathan barged in carrying Sue's stuff in a cardboard box.

He dropped the box beside Steve's desk. 'Dark horse, our Sue, there was a neat little pile of love-letters from some guy called 'Fellow Traveller' in her drawer. Deep philosophical stuff, most of it, but it got quite friendly towards the end!'

Jonathan was about to pass the letters over to Steve but Budd intercepted them. He grasped the pile and placed them carefully back in the box.

'I'll be seeing Sue. I'll look after this stuff. Make sure it's treated properly.' He glared at Jonathan, picked up the box and sauntered out, but at the door he turned and paused. 'By the way, you'd better start looking for a new photographer.'

'What's wrong with you? Got no sense of humour?' Jonathan asked innocently. But before he'd finished speaking Budd had gone. He was eager to get to the hospital to see Sue.

Father Thomas stood up and went to greet Budd as he made his way across the intensive care ward with a small bunch of flowers in his hand. Budd felt out of place and awkward. 'How is she?' he asked in a hushed whisper.

'Stable. But not good. Come and sit for a while. I'll sort out the flowers.'

Budd sank into the empty chair. He didn't look dressed for a hospital visit, but then, his wardrobe was very limited.

He leant forward and looked at Sue's pale face and her lovely fair hair against the pure white sheet. He reached forward, placed his hand around hers, and held it gently. But there was no response.

Father Thomas returned with the flowers in a plastic cup and placed them on the cabinet beside Sue's bed. They weren't neatly arranged, but they still looked beautiful. They were primroses.

'She'll like these when she wakes up,' Father Thomas said reassuringly. Budd was not optimistic that she would ever wake again, yet he hoped above hope that she would, for he had so much to say. Father Thomas placed his hand on Budd's shoulder and whispered, 'It'll all work out, you'll see,' and walked slowly down the ward. He had no wish to intrude.

A young white coated woman with a stethoscope around her neck swung into the ward. She stood looking at some charts in the far corner of the room. Budd got up and strolled over to her, looking relaxed, although he didn't feel that way.

'Hi there, I work with Sue . . . Sue Bailey. She's a friend. How's things?'

The doctor smiled a sympathetic smile. She always felt unprepared for moments such as this.

'She's very poorly. The arrhythmias have stopped now, and she's having fewer fits—but the next forty-eight hours are critical. Even if she does pull through, she's going to be a very sick lady for some time to come. She certainly knew what she was doing . . . I'd rather talk in a couple of days . . . Okay?' She turned back to her charts to cut him off, because she had no more to say.

Budd muttered a half-hearted 'Okay' and returned to

the bedside, wishing he hadn't spoken, and wondering if he should be there at all. He took a piece of paper and wrote the words 'Love from Fellow Traveller', propped it against the paper cup, and prayed that she would live.

10
Judgement Day

Budd arrived back at the *Courier* feeling bewildered and depressed. He shuddered as he walked back through reception. He would have to work out four weeks' notice, and he wondered how he'd survive the strain. He retreated to his darkroom, and the environment in which he felt secure, and picked up his drawing book.

As he drew he felt overwhelmed by despair. There was nothing he could do for Sue; no way that he could express his care for her, he could only sit and wait. He was angry that he hadn't recognised how low she'd been, and wished above all that she hadn't seen the blue envelope on his desk. He was drawing for some considerable time.

The self-portrait was complete at last. He closed the book and placed it on his desk. The decisions were made. Sue's last story had to be told, and if Steve Willshaw wouldn't use it, he'd have to find someone who would. He took out his pocket book, looked up a number, and dialled it on the phone beside his desk. He was through at once.

'Greg?' Budd asked. 'It's Budd Parkes. Remember me?'

'Well I'll be damned.' The voice was warm and friendly.

'I've got a story about a rat landlord and B&B hotels . . . black lady, two kids, lots of human interest. Good pics.'

'How can I help?'

'I'm looking for a buyer. Could you get me an intro?'

Minutes later Budd was connected to James Rand, the paper's night news editor, and was telling him Elsie's story. Within half an hour Sue's copy and Budd's prints had been faxed downtown, and Budd was back in the darkroom drawing in the leatherbound book again.

James Rand leant back on his chair and read Sue's words. It was certainly a convincing piece. But he had spiked hundreds of such stories over the years . . . they were good, but not quite good enough. Budd's pictures gave the piece extra weight and he wanted to use them if he could, but the whole piece still lacked something extra.

He turned to the shelf behind him and pulled out a file marked 'House Press Releases: Today.' He was sure he'd read of the Bourne Hotel somewhere else, but in a different context. He flicked through the pages until he found the reference to the Bourne that he'd been searching for. James Rand grinned as he dialled the number of the members' room at the Commons. Often the seemingly insignificant stories turned out to be the best of all.

Cecil Kingston was slumped in an easy chair and dozing in front of the six o'clock news on television. He was whiling away the hours in the members' lounge at the Commons until he would have to take his seat for the debate on London tourism; it was scheduled for 9pm. He'd been asked to speak about the deregulation of the hotel business, but the whip had ensured that the speech had been written for him. He didn't really trust Cecil Kingston to make a speech of his own.

It was going to be a long night. Cecil wasn't interested in the motion, and wouldn't have attended at all if the whip had not pressurised him to do so. Suddenly he heard his name, and sat up looking startled. One of the other members was calling him to the phone. He snatched the receiver.

'James Rand, Night Newsdesk Editor, the *Guardian*.'

Cecil Kingston gasped. He'd never been contacted by a national before. 'Yes?'

'I gather that you're to speak for the hotel deregulation motion tonight. Is that correct?'

Cecil Kingston swelled with pride. 'Yes, I am actually. I've got my speech here. Would you like a quote?'

'I see you've declared an interest . . .'

'Yes.' He paused. 'I own a hotel, actually.'

'How do you feel about its use as a bed and breakfast facility by social services?'

Cecil Kingston was dumbfounded. 'No comment.'

'But Mr Kingston, you must have some feelings on the matter. After all, you do own it.'

'No comment.'

'We'll run the story about Elsie Rampton as it is, then. And the pictures of the kids . . . and the squalor.'

James Rand heard a sharp intake of breath.

'How much do you know?'

The desk editor smiled a wry smile. He'd been here with other politicians before. 'Enough to embarrass you.' He was bluffing.

'But how much . . . and when are you . . . when will it be published?' Cecil Kingston's public school accent always became more accentuated when he was stressed.

'Oh, we're just finishing it off now. You'll see it in the morning.'

Cecil Kingston put down the receiver. His heart was pounding. The hotel in question had been in his family for two generations, but he'd not been near it for months. Nevertheless, he knew only too well what happened there. He'd left the running of the business in the capable hands of a manager, and all that really concerned him was the continuing income which it brought in each month.

Ten minutes later, after taking advice from Steve Willshaw at the *Courier*, Cecil Kingston called Rand back. He sounded cool and composed and knew that he needed to buy some time.

'Look here, James, thanks so much for calling me. I'd be delighted to give you an exclusive about the hotel. To be honest I've not been near the place in ages,' Cecil could really turn on the charm when he needed to. 'But give me twenty-four hours and I'll answer all the questions you want. Okay?'

The desk editor weighed his options carefully. If he ran the article without a quote it wouldn't really be strong enough, but he certainly wasn't going to tell Cecil Kingston as much. James Rand was an expert at bluffing.

'Twenty-four hours then, Mr Kingston, and you'll give me an exclusive interview? And you won't duck my questions?'

'Yes, yes.' Cecil was eager to end the conversation.

'I'll buy that.' And so the deal was struck.

Less than an hour later the two men from ADCA, Rowbottom and MacIntyre, were loading packing cases into the white high-topped transit van. Elsie and the two children stood on the pavement and watched. Steve Willshaw opened the van door and helped Elsie struggle into the high seat, and then passed the two excited children up to her. She clumsily pulled the seat belt around the three of them. James Rowbottom climbed into the driver's seat beside her.

'Time for off now, Elsie. The home of your dreams awaits you.' Steve muttered sarcastically, and then banged the door shut. He did not feel comfortable about what he was doing.

The white van drove slowly away whilst Steve and MacIntyre followed on behind in the Jaguar XJ12. It was a slow twenty-minute drive through the city before they reached the Corobridge Estate, a cheap development of high rise flats hidden away behind a large industrial estate. It had been constructed in the 1960s and exhibited all the hallmarks of a run-down overspill.

Steve escorted Elsie and the children by lift up to level six, and when they stepped out into the hallway he handed her the Yale key to flat 64B. She hurriedly turned it in the lock, the door swung open, and they all went in. Steve Willshaw switched on the lights to reveal a basic two bedroom flat which had been newly painted and carpeted. Ten year old Georgina raced over to the window 'Mam . . . come see the view . . . it's great!' Billy, meanwhile, clung tightly to his mother's blue flowered skirt.

Elsie stood beside Georgina and Billy at the window and gazed out over the grey canal to the industrial estate beyond. She could clearly see the square-shaped 'Box' which housed the *North London Courier*. It was nearly dark and she was tired. She couldn't face the cleaning job today.

'I must go now, Elsie,' said Steve, 'but don't forget to call me if you need anything. Okay?' He was doing his best to ingratiate himself. 'And please don't worry about work today.'

'Thanks mister, this'll do us fine . . .' Elsie was relieved that they had somewhere nice to live at last.

'And don't forget . . . no reporters, no statements. Just, "no comment"—agreed?'

'Of course, mister. No problem. And thanks again.'

Steve opened the door to leave and met Rowbottom and MacIntyre in the hallway with the first load of packing cases. 'Treat this lady real good. She's special. Any problems with this place . . . let me know straight away.' They muttered in agreement.

The lift was jammed with boxes so Steve clattered down the six flights of concrete steps, and the nauseating smell of stale urine filled his lungs. He couldn't wait to get out of there.

He climbed back into the XJ12 and reached for his mobile. He quickly pressed the number of the members' lounge.

'Damage limitation is now under way.' Steve sounded tense. 'The tenant has been accommodated and is happy with the arrangements. I'll have dealt with all the rest by morning. I'll call again if there is anything to report. And remember, Cecil, keep the *Courier* out of this, okay?'

Steve revved the engine and sped away. He was doing everything that he had promised to do, but there was a deep uneasiness within him which he could not quite resolve.

Rand's interview with Cecil Kingston took place in a small pub overlooking the River Thames, just beyond Tower Bridge, the following afternoon. It nestled uneasily among the renovated warehouses, an ancient structure with oak beams and whitewashed walls.

James Rand guessed that many significant conversations had taken place there across the years. It suited his purpose because it was mid-way between Docklands and Westminster, and it represented 'neutral ground' for both his victim and himself.

Cecil stared out through the leaded-light window at the grey waters of the Thames and the city skyline beyond. He fought to cover his nervousness, for he knew that this appointment could have significant implications for his future parliamentary career. Rand returned with the drinks.

James Rand took a tiny black voice recorder out of his pocket and placed it between them; he leant forward to check that the tape was running. Cecil Kingston took out a sheet of paper from his briefcase and began to speak. It was a read statement.

'Today I visited the Bourne Hotel which has been owned by my family for two generations. I was shocked to discover the appalling state of disrepair into which it has fallen. I was astonished to find the squalid conditions in which some of my constituents are living. I had no idea that whole families were being accommodated in such small rooms.'

'This afternoon I have taken steps to replace the management, and have asked the Social Services Department to remove all the families today. Elsie Rampton has been accommodated with her children in a two-bedroomed apartment at my personal expense. As soon as practicable I will sell the Bourne. I regret my own tardiness in this matter, but the pressure of constituency business has led me to neglect this area of my responsibility.'

James Rand glanced down at Susan Bailey's article which was spread out before him; and at the scribbled notes which had been phoned through from a junior reporter whom he'd dispatched to the Bourne.

'Can you tell me if you employ James Rowbottom and Bill MacIntyre?' James Rand was studying Cecil Kingston's expression carefully.

Cecil looked quickly away. 'There are so many . . . I'm not sure . . . why?'

'Very well then, let me put it this way. Do you own the "Armour Debt Collection Agency"?'

Cecil was off his prepared statement. 'What are you implying? I came to talk about the Bourne.' His public school accent was pronounced again.

'Well according to your "declaration of interests" you are the owner of ADCA, the Armour Debt Collection Agency.'

'I don't know what you're saying.' Cecil was looking out of the window again, struggling to remain cool. There was a long pause, but James Rand was in no hurry.

'Yes . . . yes . . . I own it. Okay?' Cecil was looking very worried.

'Then James Rowbottom and Bill MacIntyre are in your employ. Their names appear on the staff register. I had it checked.'

Cecil was wishing that he hadn't agreed to the interview.

'And did you know about the violence?'

'What . . .?'

'And Elsie Rampton. Is she in your employ, as well?'

'I've no idea. I really must be going. There are so many, I can't possibly know them all.'

'And would you like to put on record the hourly payment you give to Elsie Rampton for her cleaning work at the *Courier*?'

'No idea . . . this is preposterous.' Cecil got up to leave.

'Do you know the minimum pay that Ms Rampton should receive . . . according to the "low pay unit"?' James Rand was going for the kill.

'I provide jobs for people, Mr Rand. Jobs that otherwise they would not have.' Cecil Kingston was sounding very defensive.

'And why was Susan Bailey's report for the *Courier* spiked, Mr Kingston? As owner of the paper, do you often spike stories that embarrass you?'

'I think I've heard enough of your stupid insinuations. I should have known better than to trust you, Rand. These people are just trash. I've got no patience with them. Scroungers, that's what they are.'

'Just one more moment, Mr Kingston. You want to know what'll be in the paper tomorrow, don't you?'

But Cecil Kingston didn't wish to know. He stormed out without looking behind him, and climbed into his waiting taxi. James Rand sat back and finished his drink, and then he drank Kingston's full glass, too. He'd got the quote he needed, and he was more than satisfied with his afternoon's work.

That same afternoon Susan Bailey woke up. She still felt very weak and drowsy and lay motionless looking into Father Thomas's smiling blue eyes. She wasn't really sure where she was, or what had happened to her, but she found his eyes strangely reassuring.

'Everything will be fine, you'll see.' He spoke softly. She knew that she could trust him.

Heart: Everything will be fine, you'll see.
Mind: But what has changed?

And then her gaze wandered to the primroses in the paper cup, and she saw the scribbled note propped up beside them. She struggled to focus. Father Thomas took the paper. 'It just says, "Love from Fellow Traveller".'

The following morning Budd was in the darkroom looking at his photo of Susan Bailey, which was prominently displayed in the *Guardian*. He looked into her eyes and felt as miserable as hell. So this was 'Explorer', his anonymous lady.

He took a pile of letters out of his desk drawer and began to sift through them until he came across the words which haunted him.

> And so, at last, my Fellow Traveller, will you step out from the shadows and show me who you are? I long to meet you, and to see if you really are the kind of man I think you are. Perhaps now is the time for both of us to cast off our masks and to meet as real people, and to share the risk of love. Here I am, then, reaching out a hand to you as you fall through the stars—but do you care enough for me to reach back and grasp it?
>
> Explorer

Meanwhile, downstairs in the News-room, a cub reporter whistled in amazement. 'Wow guys . . . You're not going to believe this . . .'

The News-room team gathered round him and were peering at the large picture of Elsie Rampton and her children at the Bourne. At the top of the page there was a prominent head and shoulders shot of Susan Bailey. She was smiling.

'MP implicated in newspaper cover-up,' the young reporter read excitedly . . .

'Forty-five-year-old MP Cecil Kingston was having urgent talks with his constituency party today after they discovered that he had suppressed damaging information in a newspaper he owns—the *North London Courier*.

'The story, uncovered by *Courier* reporter Sue Bailey, implicated Mr Kingston in running a debt collection agency which used violent methods on a number of the MP's constituents.

'It also revealed that he is proprietor of a bed and breakfast hotel which health officials today described as "uninhabitable". Asked about his reaction to the allegations Cecil Kingston told me "These people are just trash. I've got no patience with them. Scroungers, that's what they are."'

Meanwhile Steve Willshaw was out in the carpark. He was loading boxes of personal papers into the open boot of his Jaguar XJ12. He had no intention of becoming the fall guy for Cecil Kingston.

11
The Bonfire

Sue's recovery was a lengthy process. After two days in intensive care and eight days in a general ward she was ready to begin her convalescence. Father Thomas arranged for her to be transferred to a community called the 'Sisters of Charity' which was situated on the outskirts of a picturesque Dorset village. Sue needed some time to think, and Father Thomas was very persuasive.

'It'll do you the world of good, Susan,' he promised. 'It's lovely down there, and they won't put you under pressure to do anything.'

The four weeks which Sue spent at 'Tumbledown', as the old house was known, turned out to be some of the richest days of her life. The landscaped grounds were filled with daffodils and primroses, and the mild spring days seemed full of hope. Sue still felt physically weak and she was often in tears, but there was an exhilaration about being alive which she'd not known since childhood.

The simplest of things filled her with joy, yellow daffodils, spring lambs, the first buds on the trees, pure white clouds, and the soft rain. She'd forgotten what a joy it was to walk through gentle rain, and to feel the moisture covering her face.

Her tiny room overlooked a rustic farmyard, and during her early days at Tumbledown she sat by the window for hours on end, mesmerised by the tranquil scene. In one corner of the cobbled yard there was a great pile of kindling wood, and in another a very old tractor which never moved, and everywhere there were hens strutting this way and that.

There was a steady routine in the farmyard from early cock-crow and the arrival of the cows each morning to the occasional hoot of a barn owl at night. Sue found it all comforting and reassuring.

There was a strong routine within Tumbledown, as well. At six am each morning Sister Catherine, a young novice, would climb up the rickety wooden stairs to the small bell-tower beside the gable-end and ring the bell three times for 'Angelus'. Sue would lie in bed and listen as the seven Sisters of Charity assembled in the small chapel at the end of her corridor. She would hear the soft tones of the harmonium drifting across to her, followed, shortly afterwards, by the sweet harmony of voices knit together by years of companionship. As she lay there the peace and security of Tumbledown enfolded her.

The Mother Superior had lived at Tumbledown for nearly fifty years, but she still knew how to make her guests feel truly welcome. Sister Anna was in her early eighties, and crippled with arthritis. She managed to shuffle about Tumbledown with a walking stick, but her progress was exceedingly slow and evidently painful. Her office was situated beside the panelled hallway, and her door was always open.

'Susan, my dear,' she had said on the day that Sue arrived, 'we are here to serve you, but not to suffocate you . . . we will respect your privacy, but welcome you to share our life here in whatever way may please you . . .'

Sue looked into Sister Anna's puddle grey eyes, and read there the suffering and pain which the arthritis had brought her. 'I just need some space to think . . . and some time to find a way ahead,' she said softly.

The elderly nun, clothed in her black habit, leant forward on the high-backed wooden chair. Her wrinkled face was full of understanding. 'You'll find that Tumbledown will give you all the space you need . . .' She paused, as if to add something profound, and whispered enthusiastically, 'We've never had an agony aunt staying here before.' She beamed. 'Maybe you could sort us out while you're here.'

After the first few days, walking became an important part of Sue's daily routine. She would take the narrow overgrown footpath past the farmyard and the two thatched cottages and out along the country road to Brimshill Spinney. She'd cross the grassy meadow, past Copplemore barn and up the slight incline known locally as Highlands.

At the top of the hill was a disused windmill built of stone, its broken cross-shaped wooden arms silhouetted against the sky. The view from the windmill was breathtaking. Sue would stand and look back across the meadows toward the distant shape of Tumbledown, and feel in some strange way that she belonged. Then she'd continue over the brow of the hill and follow the shadowy path through Sywell Wood, emerging at the rough grassy clearing near the clifftop. The fresh breeze rolling off the sea exhilarated her, and she'd often run down the twisting cliff path to the deserted beach below.

Sue spent hours down at the seashore. It was the sea which thrilled her most, and especially the angry waves crashing onto the shingly beach. She loved the crunch of the shingle beneath her feet, the fresh salty smell of the sea air, and the excited sounds of screeching seagulls overhead. Here was freedom to walk. Here was time to think. Here was space to be. Life, it seemed, was after all worth the living.

Although the Sisters met in the chapel for prayer several times each day, they did not invite Sue to share with them. Gradually, Sue became fascinated by this most private part of their life together and she would listen to their hushed whispers from the safety of her own room, with the door slightly ajar.

The seven nuns who made up the community at Tumbledown were all elderly, save Catherine, the young Bradford girl who wore the white veil of a novice. Catherine was working on her own in the vegetable garden when Sue first approached her. 'Are you allowed to talk?'

Catherine smiled behind her veil. 'Of course I am! This isn't a prison!' she paused. 'I could join you for your walk if you like . . . but I'd have to tell Sister Anna first.'

So began a daily pattern. When Catherine had finished her work, and had said her midday prayers, the two women would walk together down Sue's familiar path.

Catherine was not a bit as Sue had imagined her. She was twenty-six, well read, good humoured, and in touch with the real world. Once they had walked beyond the thatched houses Catherine would talk freely, even excitedly, in her broad Yorkshire accent. She shared deeply and honestly about anything and everything. As they walked they told the stories of their lives, and by what strange and different paths they had arrived at the quaint old house called Tumbledown.

Catherine had trained in accountancy, passed all her examinations, and then suddenly realised that she had done it all to please her domineering father. After much inner turmoil, she had decided to cut a different path for herself, and the life of the Sisters of Charity was the path of sacrifice she'd chosen.

Catherine had known love, too, but for her the decision to enter Tumbledown was not a reaction to heartbreak. She had sensed a growing conviction that she was wasting her life in accountancy and that she would only find fulfilment in complete surrender to her Lord.

'But why the Sisters of Charity . . . and why Tumbledown?' As Sue listened to herself she knew that she was still a reporter at heart.

'Oh, Tumbledown is just the first step along the way,' sighed Catherine. 'I hope to end up in Africa, Tanzania, actually. We have a hospital there.'

Sue sighed. 'But why . . . why do you do it?'

'"Whose feet will you wash? For whom will you care? In comparison with whom will you be the least?" . . . Basil, he wrote that.'

'Basil? Basil who?'

Catherine turned to her. 'He's an Early Church Father, have you never heard of . . . well I guess not, maybe it's time I introduced you to him and the others. They're all in the library if you're interested.' Sue nodded. She was remembering something Father Thomas had said.

As they stood by the windmill one misty day and looked at the bell-tower poking through the haze, Catherine turned to Sue and asked, almost apologetically, 'Why don't you join us for Compline?'

Sue smiled. 'Compline? It sounds like a health drink!'

Catherine giggled. 'Yes, it does! But it is more of a bed-time drink, actually. Compline is prayers before bed! It'll help you sleep better.'

Sue smiled. 'Thanks . . . I'd like to come.'

At eight-thirty each evening the Sisters gathered in their chapel, and Sue joined them. She sat alone in the back row more an observer than a participant, but they didn't seem to mind.

The letters from Budd came each day. They were very short and factual at first, but gradually, as Budd received Sue's replies, they became more confident and personal. As they grew in intensity she came to treasure them. They were the most beautiful letters she'd ever received. She would sit expectantly around coffee-time every morning and wait for the post-van to arrive.

Every evening after Compline, Sue would sit alone at the old oak table in the Tumbledown library with its leathery smell of old books. Under the light of an old desk lamp with a green glass shade, she would pour out her heart to Budd in reply. She wrote letters about life, about love, and the joy of caring and being cared for. Here, she felt, was someone who understood the complexities of her human spirit. Here was someone who would not judge her, condemn her or belittle her, but whose love would liberate her. In his company her spirit would grow, and in his compassion she would regain the sense of direction she had lost.

Budd's letters enabled her to dismantle, piece by piece, the wall of depression which had separated her from the world. He wrote with a profound understanding of suffering, and with a compassion which had been deepened by sorrow.

Budd wrote of his love for Maria Hampton, and of the pain and torment he'd known since her death. He described how, through his sorrow, he had come to understand the reality of heaven; and how a priest called Father Thomas had helped him to find a sense of God's presence in his wilderness of despair.

And Catherine was right. The prayers of Compline were some of the most healing that she'd ever heard. Night after night Sister Anna would repeat them in just the same way in her weak lilting voice; and as night followed night in the ordered pattern of life at Tumbledown Sue slowly entered into their meaning.

'. . . protect us through the silent hours of this night . . . that we who are wearied by the changes and chances of this fleeting world . . . may rest upon your eternal changelessness . . .'

The words of Compline slowly became a part of her being, and they began to follow her like a shadow. In the darkness of her small room, with the distant hooting of the barn owl the lovely words 'rest upon your eternal changelessness' would return to soothe her.

By the windmill one day . . . 'Be for me a rock of refuge, a fortress to defend me; for you are my high rock, and my stronghold . . .'

And standing in Brimshill Spinney and watching a bird feeding its young . . . 'He will cover you with his wings, and you will be safe under his feathers; his faithfulness will be your shield and defence.'

And racing down the cliff path . . . 'Where could I go to escape from you? Where could I get away from your presence? If I went up to heaven, you would be there; if I lay down in the world of the dead, you would be there . . .'

And crunching over the damp shingly beach, and looking out at the grey sea which melted into the grey sky over the far horizon . . . 'if I flew away beyond the east or lived in the farthest place in the west, you would be there to lead me, you would be there to help me . . .'

And watching the swirling seagulls overhead which were never still and never silent; 'Come to me all you who labour and are heavy laden, and I will give you rest . . .'

Sue began to browse through the books in the library. They were books the like of which she'd never seen before, let alone read. Books by Cyprian, and Thomas Aquinas, and by the Early Church Fathers. This was not light reading, but between these faded covers were words full of healing for Sue's bruised spirit. Words older than fifteen centuries. Words locked in long unopened leatherbound books covered in dust. Words so rich in meaning that they tasted as intoxicating as strong sweet wine. She was overcome by their intensity.

Sometimes a phrase or a prayer would hold her gripped in a timeless haze in the shadowy darkness of the Tumbledown library. 'Not the wide bounds of earth nor the kingdoms of this world will avail me anything . . .' The words of Ignatius.

Sometimes the words would set her heart racing with excitement, as though she had discovered the key to everything. 'All that abides . . . abides in You alone . . .

the movement of the universe surges towards You . . . of all beings You are the goal.' Gregory.

Sometimes the words baffled her and she longed to understand them more completely, 'The life came down that he might be slain . . . the bread came down that he might hunger . . . the way came down that he might grow weary on the way . . . the fount came down that he might thirst . . .' Augustine.

Sometimes the words were so precious that she'd scribble them in her diary, and take them with her on her daily walks with Catherine.

As they stood together on the shingly beach one day and watched the waves crashing in, Sue spoke aloud her scribbled quotations of Cyprian, shouting them at the sea.

'I lay prostrate in the shadows of a pitch-dark night, and was tossed to and fro on the waves of this troubled world, ignorant of my true life, a stranger to life and truth . . . then, in a marvellous way I saw certainty remove my doubts, barriers open, the darkness lighten, that which had once seem difficult now prove easy . . .'

Sue turned to Catherine. 'I want this, Catherine . . . I want this with all my being . . . where do I go to find it?'

Catherine's face was clearly visible. The sea breeze was blowing her veil to the side. 'Gregory said . . . "no matter where you may be, as long as your soul forms the sort of resting place in which God can dwell and linger, He will visit you."'

After three weeks, with the agreement of Sister Anna, Budd came to stay for the weekend at Tumbledown. It was the most beautiful weekend of her life. They walked and walked, for she wanted to share with him the narrow footpaths, and to stand beside him in the secret places of beauty she'd discovered during her days of convalescence.

They talked as though they'd been friends for a lifetime. They shared the deep secrets of their hearts and tracked back and forward through the memories of the years. They were catching up on each other's lives.

She told him about the death of her father, and the childhood pain it caused her, and her fear of caring. She told him of Pete and of the hopes she'd had for loving him, of the growing sense of distance she'd felt between them, and of the girl she'd glimpsed in his flat that fateful day.

He told her of his love for Maria, and of the devastation of her death, and all the broken dreams. And the long dark months of mourning.

And late at night they sat at the table in the musty library, where Sue had written so many of her deepest thoughts to him, and they talked of God. Budd's faith had developed from early childhood in a home shaped by believing parents, but it was a faith which had been sorely tried and tested through his loss of Maria. Had it not been for Father Thomas he'd have probably lost his faith for ever.

Father Thomas had suggested that he chart his journey through the grief, and had given him a thick leather-bound book in which to do so. Budd placed it carefully on the table and pulled the old green desk lamp towards him so that its light illumined the pages. He'd never shown it to anyone before. It documented in graphic detail the dark road that he'd been travelling.

There were pictures of hands, and faces, and trees and crosses. And of the eyes of Jesus . . . drawn again and again, as if he was trying to get them right.

'What do they all mean?' Sue whispered, overwhelmed by their intensity.

'You're into words, aren't you? These words you're always quoting, Cyprian, and Augustine? But I'm into pictures, and that's how God speaks to me.'

Sue paused at each page and wondered at the power of the grief they conveyed. The early pictures following

Maria's death were of wild dark eyes clinging on to life, and of Christ's broken body on the cross and his face dominated by the same wild eyes. And beneath the pictures there were words and phrases from the Bible. 'My God, my God, why have you abandoned me?'

But there were other pictures, too. A wilderness, a path and cacti . . . and a scorching sun. And a lone figure struggling onward, his eyes dark with despair. Beneath, in Budd's familiar handwriting were the words of Job. 'Month after month I have nothing to live for; night after night brings me grief. When I lie down to sleep, the hours drag; I toss all night and long for dawn . . . Remember, O God, my life is only a breath; my happiness has already ended.'

Budd slowly turned the page, but he didn't speak. A man was falling through the universe, as if out of control. His hand grasping out for safety and his eyes pleading for help. And underneath the words of the psalmist . . . 'Let my cry for help reach you, Lord. Give me understanding, as you have promised.'

Budd gently turned the page again, but this time it was clear that the man was Budd, and he was not alone . . . there was another figure beside him. It was the figure of Christ and he had eyes like those of Father Thomas. And underneath, in black ink, 'He will wipe away all the tears from their eyes . . .'

On the Saturday night at Tumbledown they sat together in the little chapel and shared in Compline and, as the old harmonium played and the familiar words were spoken, he leant over and gently took her hand in his. She held it tight, and listened to his soft voice as he recited the words of Compline '. . . that we, who are wearied by the changes and chances of this fleeting world, may rest upon your eternal changelessness . . .' And she knew that, somehow, in the mystery of God, they had become fellow travellers.

Father Thomas stood beside a large bonfire in the back garden of his small retirement cottage. The smoke was billowing in the gentle breeze.

Sue Bailey stood watching him, but he didn't notice. He was staring into the flames as though intrigued by the shapes they formed. She felt she owed this man a debt of gratitude that she could never repay.

Suddenly he turned and noticed her. 'Susan! How lovely to see you back!' He strode towards her, his blue eyes shining with joy, 'You look so well. Radiant.'

'I am well, Tom. Thanks to you.'

'Me? Why's that?'

'You've been praying for me. I know it.'

Father Thomas smiled. 'Come over to the fire.'

They both stood beside the fire and warmed their hands. It crackled, and the smoke rising from the branches smelt of apples. Father Thomas picked up a cardboard box and poured its contents onto the fire. Letters, cheque book stubs, church magazines, and some old photos.

'What's all this then? Been clearing out?' Sue's fair hair was unkempt, blown about by the breeze.

'Yes, moving to a smaller place makes you work out what you really need. But I've taken it a lot further.'

Sue smiled. There was a long smear of charcoal down Tom's cheek. She took out a paper handkerchief, wet it with her lips, and wiped the stain away.

'I've been packing my bags for eternity.'

Sue smiled again. 'That sounds a bit dramatic, Tom. You're not leaving us just yet, are you?'

He turned, his blue eyes shining with joy. 'Well, perhaps not just yet, but I really don't mind when.'

'So, what do you mean . . . packing your bags for . . .'

'Remember when you came to interview me?' Sue nodded, and brushed back her hair. 'You made me look back over my life again, with all your probing questions—and I began to see that I'd been carrying around all kinds of junk, junk that's useless for this life and an encumbrance in the next . . .'

He took another cardboard box from the grass beside him. 'So . . . here it goes . . . all that stuff that's been filling my life . . . and keeping my mind fixed on the kingdoms of this world . . . instead of the one Kingdom. The Kingdom of God.'

'I've got some stuff to chuck on there, too.'

Father Thomas beamed a great smile. 'Have you Sue, really?'

'Remember Augustine's prayer? "Late have I loved you, beauty so old and so new, late have I loved you" . . .' Sue whispered.

Father Thomas turned to her, his blue eyes glistening with tears and together they prayed 'You were within me, and I was outside. There I sought you, You touched me, and your peace has saved me . . .'

He picked up an old spade from the grass beside him and poked the fire to let the air inside. The flames leapt up again and some of the smouldering papers fell out onto the grass. He beat the flames with the end of the spade, and then leant on it. Sue stooped to pick up one of the charred fragments.

'Remind you of anything?' Sue showed him the paper. Father Thomas laughed. It was a scorched picture of him in a garden, leaning on a spade.

'Well, maybe the article was right after all.' He lay the spade down again.

Sue folded the photo and placed it carefully in her pocket. 'Right?'

'I am happy now, happier than for a very long time.'

'You're enjoying gardening then?'

'There's a bigger garden to tend than this one, Sue, and I've found my place in it again.' He took a third box and cast its contents over the crackling wood. The flames seemed to leap up to greet them. 'So you've some rubbish to burn as well?'

'Yes . . . plenty . . . I had it all the wrong way round, didn't I? Before, life was all for me . . . but now, it's all for Him.'

'Then throw them all on, Susan Bailey . . . let them go . . . all those questions which were ripping you apart . . . and see how they burn . . . because now you have the answer!' And he let out an enormous 'Hallelujah!' Then, taking both her hands in his, he danced her round the bonfire. And they laughed and laughed until they could laugh no more.

The old church beside the canal was full of flowers. There were flowers at every window, and the altar was carpeted with daffodils. The church was hushed and crowded, and the old organ was playing softly.

The congregation stood. Paula, the bridesmaid, lifted the veil and kissed Sue gently. 'Good luck, kid. I'm so happy for you . . .' She straightened the veil, and Susan Bailey walked gracefully down the long stone aisle toward Budd, who had turned to greet her.

Father Thomas smiled his warm smile as he watched her approaching. She was carrying a beautiful posy of yellow primroses. And on her arm was a nun dressed all in black, save for a white veil. 'Who gives this woman to be married to this man . . .?' Sister Catherine stepped forward and momentarily lifted her veil. 'I do.'

Budd and Sue both knelt, and Father Thomas took a piece of bread and handed it to the groom. He took it, and first gave it to his wife, saying 'The Body of Christ'. She took the remainder from him and placed it in his open hand . . . 'The body of Christ'.

Father Thomas held his hands outspread over them as if in blessing and declared, 'This is a foretaste of the heavenly banquet.' His blue eyes were shining with joy, for indeed everything had worked out right, in the end.

When Budd kissed the bride it was the longest kiss ever seen in a wedding service; so long, in fact, that the gang from the *Courier* led the congregation in a thunderous round of applause. And someone, whom Sue suspected to be Jonathan, let out an enormous wolf-whistle.

Kingsway